MORGANA ENRAGED

MORGANA ENRAGED

WITCH OF THE FEDERATION™ BOOK 04

MICHAEL ANDERLE

DISRUPTIVE IMAGINATION

Copyright © 2019 Michael Anderle
Cover copyright © LMBPN Publishing
Cover Art by Jake @ J Caleb Design
http://jcalebdesign.com / jcalebdesign@gmail.com
A Michael Anderle Production

LMBPN Publishing
PMB 196, 2540 South Maryland Pkwy
Las Vegas, NV 89109

Version 1.00, November 2021
Previously Published as part of the megabook *Witch Of The Federation II*
ebook ISBN: 978-1-68500-618-1
Print ISBN: 978-1-68500-619-8

THE MORGANA ENRAGED TEAM

Thanks to our Beta Team

Crystal Wren, Daniel Weigert, James Caplan, John Ashmore, Larry Omans, Mary Morris, Nicole Emens, and Robert Brooks

Thanks to our JIT Readers

Angel LaVey
Daniel Weigert
Dave Hicks
Diane L. Smith
Dorothy Lloyd
Jeff Eaton
Jeff Goode
John Ashmore
Larry Omans
Misty Roa

If We've missed anyone, please let us know!

Editor
The Skyhunter Editing Team

To Family, Friends and
Those Who Love
To Read.
May We All Enjoy Grace
To Live The Life We Are
Called.

CHAPTER ONE

"It's like she's a completely different person to the young girl described in the folder," Corporal Host told the recruiting team. They had gathered to discuss their meeting with Stephanie, which hadn't gone well.

The corporal tapped the end of his pen on the mahogany table as he scanned his notes from the meeting. "Seriously, during the interview, she was calm and quiet, reserved even. Like she had a handle on the whole goddamned world. We have forty-year officers who break a sweat easier than that. We need that kind of calmness in our ranks."

"That and her knowledge," Holland pointed out. "She is full of information about how to use magic, and I don't even understand how she has it. She has never set foot on Meligorn."

"She has a teacher from there," Brown replied.

"So?" Holland sneered. "The shit she pulled at the Gala had nothing to do with any teacher she might have had. That's the kind of thing you would only know from personal experience. From the notes you gave me, Corporal, it sounds like you talked to a sixty-year-old professor of magic, not some kid from the Gov-Subs."

Petty Officers Grant, Taylor, and Chavez walked into the room and sat wearily. The team still looked half-dead from the last shift they'd pulled. Holland slid the report across the table to them. "This is Corporal Host. He's here to give us a briefing on the meeting with Stephanie Morgana. We're only waiting on the LT to arrive."

"So what's new? We're always waiting on Conrad." Chavez yawned.

"Unlike you slackers, I actually have responsibilities," the man in question said as he stepped through the door, bright-eyed. Everyone stood while he shook Host's hand and then claimed their seats.

Chavez offered Conrad the file, but the Lieutenant shook his head. "I've already read it, although I'm not sure why any of this came as a surprise to you. The girl has just had the fight of her life and is recovering. She is under Meligornian protection right now. We're the last people she would want to see. Nonetheless, Corporal, let's hear your breakdown."

Host leaned forward and cleared his throat nervously. "When we arrived at the ambassador's temporary residence, we met with some resistance from the security chief, Brilgus. He tried to fob us off, but we were able to insist on seeing her as a matter of national security, so we waited. It took about forty minutes before Stephanie arrived. She looked extremely weak, as was to be expected."

Thompkins scoffed and pushed back an annoying strand of hair that had fallen from her near-perfect bun. "She'd just finished taking down more than a dozen would-be assassins and healing people with her hands. Tired is the least I would be."

"True," Host replied. "When we got through telling her about her career options—you know, the normal stuff—she thought about it for only a moment. Her response was adamant but didn't seem rehearsed or coerced. She said she felt it wasn't time for her to move from her 'existing role.' She didn't want to be tied down by a three-year contract, or to study magic under military constraints."

Conrad hadn't been surprised in the least by the maturity of Stephanie's response. "She has worked with powerful people. You saw how she was at the Gala. She is obviously not the immature little girl everyone wants to think she is." He paused and looked around the room. "How did our normal tactics to counter the arguments about the contract time and military research restrictions work?"

Host shook his head and his fingers massaged the tender skin on his temples. "They didn't. We were only alone with her for the first part of the conversation. We couldn't refuse to allow anyone in the room if she wanted them there, so when she requested the ambassador's attendance, we were essentially screwed."

Thompkins clicked her tongue and shook her head as she leaned back with her arms folded. "That's some bullshit right there. I'm sorry, but there was no reason for him to want to be there. He should have been minding his damn business elsewhere. She is not a minor anymore. She can make her own choices."

Host waved his hand. "No, it's not that she took his advice or felt threatened by the glare of his Meligornian eyes or anything. She had already stated very clearly that she was not interested. What the ambassador's presence prevented us from doing was to attempt to manipulate her into enlisting or push half-truths about what a career with us would be like. You know, the typical bullshit we use to make the job sound glamorous and perfect."

Conrad uncrossed his legs, leaned forward, and intertwined his fingers. "It's not as if that would have worked on her anyway."

Chavez shook his head. "I don't understand, Conrad. Why do you want to enlist this girl so badly?"

Their commanding officer flipped the file open to a picture of the aftermath of the assassination attempt at the Gala. He pointed to the crack in the marble stairs where the ambassador and Stephanie had made their stand and stared at Chavez. "That's why. Because this girl is not only incredibly intelligent but whatever magic she uses, she is far more adept at it than any witch I've seen. This is not normal Meligornian magic. There is something else twisted through the strands of energy she uses. This girl is unlike any magic user we have ever come across, and I am tired of us acting like she is merely some ordinary person. That is why our usual recruiting tactics didn't work."

Host nodded and wiped his forehead, even though there didn't seem to be a glimmer of sweat on his brow. "She has a solid head on her shoulders, that's for sure, and between that and her support system, I don't see how we could even come close to convincing her to enlist. I even attempted to talk up boot camp and she simply smiled and listened but didn't really pay any attention. When I was done, she pointed out how long someone spent in boot camp versus actual service in the military, the percentages and statistics tied to injury and death, and the amount of time she would actually have to fulfill her purpose there. It was almost like she had some damned AI whispering in her ear."

His lips pursed, Conrad flipped through the file before he retrieved a flash drive from his pocket. He stood and walked over to the screen to insert the drive into a slot before he clicked it on. The images flickered out to form a 3D effect.

He swiped his hand across the device a few times until he came to a frame taken from the media footage of the battle at the Gala.

"Watch this clip of the fight," he instructed and pressed play.

The others focused on the screen as Stephanie hurled magic in controlled attacks to eliminate one would-be assassin after another. Her magic brought chunks of marble down onto one attacker and blasted through others before the scene skipped to her healing the other defenders. Conrad paused it and pointed at one aspect. "There! Do you see that?"

He transferred the image from the screen to the small mounted box in the center of the table, enlarged it, and walked around the table so the others could have a better view. Chavez leaned in and narrowed his eyes. "Her magic is different there than it was during the fight." He cocked his head for a moment and allowed his brain to catch up to what he saw. "Actually, it seems purer there, while the fight contains a mixture."

"Exactly," Host said and chuckled. "Impressive. It took our guys several days to even notice that—and this is why we're trying to recruit her. When we realized she wasn't interested in hearing the positives and negatives of a military career, we switched gears. We wanted to find out what information we could get from her. It soon became obvious she had absolutely no intention to help us by spilling everything she knew."

Conrad glanced quickly at him. "What did you get from her?" he asked, his interest piqued.

Host flipped through his notes, licked his thumb, and turned the pages until he found what he was looking for. "She admitted to the use of something called Earth MU, which she called eMU or 'light' magic. Also, she said she used Meligornian magic from normal MU batteries. She wouldn't confirm or deny knowing of, or using, any other types."

Petty Officer Taylor put his hands up in the air. "Hold up. Wait a second. Are you telling me that she was able to pull enough of this mythical Earth Energy—the shit we thought only existed in stories—and use it for real? Like she pumped it through her veins?"

Conrad smirked. "Interesting, huh? She is definitely doing something new, something more than merely being sensitive to MU."

"Yeah, and we think there is a substantial amount of research behind it, too, but how much, we don't know," Host stated. "The problem is, if it does exist, the information probably belongs to ONE R&D because that's who she works for. Obviously, we'll put in a request with them to learn more. However, they are clearly a major player, even though it's the first time I've heard of them. I'm sure politics will have to play a role in this one—especially with the Meligornians involved."

Conrad stared off into the distance as he rocked back on his chair and rubbed his chin. He grinned slightly. "I guess we'll have to wait and see. Hopefully, not for too long."

Across the city, in the security of her room at the Meligornian ambassador's residence, Stephanie stared out the window. Her thoughts wandered and she thought about how lucky she was.

For as long as she could remember, she'd dreamt of Meligorn —of the purple haze surrounding the planet, the clouds, the moons, and most of all, the magic.

She'd dreamt of a richness of enchantment so thick that she could stand still in the spiraling, rocketing universe and watch the magic billow out around her.

As a child, her imagination had run wild and she daydreamed of the way the warm Meligornian air mixed with the MU native to the world to create a powerful well of witchery deep inside her.

When she'd been growing up, with every day that had passed leading up to her testing, Stephanie had thought of Earth as dull and lackluster. The dense smoke undulating into the grey sky overshadowed the already gloomy Gov-Subs and colored the perceptions of those who lived there.

The people who trudged to and from work or simply counted down the hours and minutes of life as they rocked meaninglessly on their porches dragged at her. The heaviness was fueled by the paint peeling from the buildings and fences, and the babies' cries that echoed through the silence of the poor and destitute areas of the country.

Beneath that smog and despair, however, was something Stephanie had never paid any attention to.

Instead of looking up toward Meligorn, she realized she should have kept a steady eye on her very own home. Radiating from the torched and empty landscapes around her was a magic all their own. Faint or invisible to the unknowing but strong for her, Earth's light magic, or eMU, was worth trying to channel.

Stephanie sat quietly, as she had since the battle at the Arts Gala. She continued to stare at the cityscape beyond her room at the ambassador's residence. She'd had him remove the outside enchantment that masked the city from view but retained those that protected everyone inside the residence.

She wanted to see her home planet but still clung to the childish whimsy of a castle bedroom—the perfect existence of a princess, even one locked in a tower. When she looked outside, though, her eyes quickly adjusted, and she saw everything she had ignored for years.

It surprised her that she could watch three different types of energy moving and swaying as though the Earth breathed and it had to keep time. She saw the purple energy of Meligorn, even though it was rare and only visible as trails from Meligornian visitors or the odd human who carried a battery as they moved about the streets.

The blue energy, though, was prominent. It was Earth's very own MU field, a radiance of bright rays and swirls of color like ink in water. The eMU seemed equally as strong as the MU she felt when she visited Meligorn inside the virtual world, even though she knew that couldn't be true. eMU, in essence, was never that strong.

Beyond the blues and purples, beyond the wavering winds, was a third energy. She had decided to call it gMU because she'd seen it mixed with MU from Meligorn, and she could see it mixed with eMU, so it had to be galaxy-wide, a kind of Galaxy MU.

She liked that.

This gMU glowed faintly silver, almost invisible in nature and very, very weak. She guessed that if you weren't trained to look for it—or weren't really, really sensitive to MU like she was—you could go your whole life and never know it was there.

But she could see it creeping through the other energy and dancing the Earth's sweet dance. It was almost entrancing.

Behind her, the door opened and Stephanie's concentration broke. She sighed as the magic faded from view and turned as the ambassador entered.

"Do you still see the energy?" he asked.

She looked briefly at the window and nodded. "This third type of energy I told you about, it seems so...out of place, yet familiar, like it belongs with everything. I want to know if it's stronger out in space."

He gave her a kind smile and his robes brushed the floor as he walked toward her. "You will have time to explore it. I came to give you your doctor's release."

Stephanie turned, took the paper, and grinned at him. They both chuckled over the irony that she'd had to wait for an Earthbound human doctor to say she was well enough to return to work at Burt's compound. Her magic was so strong and she'd needed special Meligornian care to recover from the after-effects of using so much magic at the Gala that a human opinion actually seemed irrelevant. Still, it was what it was, and her manager, Ms. E, wouldn't let her budge a muscle until that paper had been signed.

It was peace of mind for everyone, Stephanie supposed.

The ambassador lifted a piece of her hair. The strain of using so much magic had mostly manifested as overwhelming fatigue, but there had been one lasting physical effect.

When she saw him inspect the white streaks that ran to the ends of her hair, she chuckled nervously and pulled it out of his grasp. "I haven't dyed it yet. I think I might like being the sexiest-looking white-haired old lady on the street."

A smile curved V'ritan's lips. He tucked his hands in his sleeves and glanced out the window. "I am waiting for a response from my king on a couple of matters. Of course, nothing happens in a timely fashion when it comes to government. Apparently, it doesn't matter what planet you live on, this one truth is universal."

Stephanie laughed, walked over to her dresser, and gathered a couple of things. She hadn't been out in what seemed like forever, and the eMU that radiated from below had teased her almost deliberately. The ambassador watched as she made her preparations.

"I want to make sure you are careful down there. Remember that eMU is not the same as Meligornian magic, and there are so many things that could go wrong. I'm sure you feel much more magic now that your channels have opened."

"It's strange," she replied and paused her task to stare off into the distance. "I can see it all around me. I can feel its power. What I need to do is learn how to let it flow into me and learn to control it. That will probably be my greatest need. God knows what I'd do if it overflowed."

"We might find you in pieces," the ambassador half-joked. "Oh, and so you know, I'm following up with the Federation Navy."

Stephanie rolled her eyes. "Do they always recruit so forcefully and then demand information that is really not their business when they fail?"

V'ritan loved her spark—her sass, as Ms. E called it—and it only seemed to have grown since the fight.

With a smirk, he shook his head. "No. They don't. It wasn't an appropriate request to make of you. I've seen them act similarly in the past toward other people they hoped to acquire. I think they are up to something."

"Probably because they can't simply acquire humans. We aren't objects," she snipped.

The ambassador drew a deep breath. "Unfortunately, the Federation doesn't feel that way. To them, everything is obtainable. Everything can be an asset and vice versa."

Stephanie shrugged. "What will they do? Conscript me?"

He pursed his lips and his gaze slid to the side.

She looked at him with shock and tossed her hands up in the air with a sigh. "Great."

Brilgus walked into the room, wiping his hands on a towel. "Are you packing?"

The tension left her shoulders and she looked at the bodyguard, who had worked his butt off as a housemaid even though he was head of security and her team tried to clean up after themselves as best they could.

"I have the all-clear, my friend. I gotta get back to the bunker and do more research. I've taken my time healing, and it's time I stopped being a lazy ass and got shit done. Right?"

Brilgus shrugged but didn't seem too fond of the idea. The ambassador put his hand on the security chief's shoulder and chuckled. "Of course it is. A bright explorer and scientist like yourself cannot simply wait around. But remember not to push yourself too hard."

Stephanie shouldered her bag, walked to the door, and rested her hand on the doorframe. She paused and turned to them. "Would you care to join me for dinner sometime soon?"

The two men exchanged glances, and V'ritan nodded. "We would never turn you down but had thought that with as much as we put you through, you might want to steer clear of us for a while, at least in public."

She tilted her head as she regarded them steadily, the crisp white ends to her hair obvious against her black top. "I can choose to run, or I can choose to embrace my future. I'm a Morgana. I don't run from anything."

Brilgus laughed deeply. "Is that the house motto?"

"It should be," she said with a wink. "And as a matter of a fact, it is now."

When she made it to the front of the house, the team was ready and waiting for her. Lars reached over and took her bag and Ms. Elizabeth wrapped her arm around Stephanie's shoulders. "Are you ready to get back home?"

Stephanie gave her a half smile. "Yep. As long as the guys are ready to get an ass-whooping in training."

Johnny scoffed and tapped her on the top of the head. "While you've lounged around pretending to watch magic, we've trained to kick your butt."

She laughed at the jokes and enjoyed the sense of camaraderie they shared. Ms. E cleared her throat and they all fell silent and turned to face the ambassador and Brilgus. She put her hand to her chest and bowed. "Thank you for everything you have done. You have been kinder than we could ever have imagined."

V'ritan bowed back. "It is our pleasure. Anything for Stephanie Morgana."

He winked at Stephanie as he turned to walk out of the room. Lars nudged her in the back and chuckled as he stage-whispered. "Fan club. Why didn't I get an invite?"

They all turned to leave, and she nudged him in return. "Because it's only for winners, not slackers."

The laughter that filled the space as they left was pleasant, much needed, and had been absent for too long.

>>CROSS REFERENCE: STEPHANIE MORGANA

BURT clicked through his system and searched for all the news about Stephanie—the battle, the magic, and basically, anything else he could get his virtual hands on.

He wanted to keep up with how the world viewed her and

what type of attention she would receive on an ongoing basis. Things had largely settled since the battle, but there was still a significant load of new articles and reports on her.

She hadn't faded from the public eye yet, and he wasn't sure that she ever would. After all, she was the Federation's witch, although the Federation struggled to gain control of her.

From what he could determine, research into her background was performed without being signaled by his system. They had discovered that Stephanie had not been picked for the top two percent of graduate opportunities. Of course, BURT was a valued member of the website and used different names as cover.

On this particular instance, he had chosen to log in as The Iron Lady—a play on the historical Margaret Thatcher, of course.

He went to work and typed a reply, using the persona of a relatively strong-willed reader who dug in when it came to equal opportunity among the classes.

This doesn't seem to be accurate or fair. If she is the most powerful human or one of the most powerful in history, how does she not make the top 2%? This doesn't seem fair and definitely appears to be some kind of political screw.

Happy with his comment, BURT moved on and continued his search for how to tap in to find others like Stephanie who needed to be tagged for his company's efforts.

He had computed the odds of her being the only one capable of research on a scale which would advance them and found the likelihood to be very remote. There might not be another witch, but that didn't mean there weren't more incredibly intelligent students who would never see the advantage of a prep-school campus.

As he searched, his system discovered additional research. The information immediately triggered a warning and he took a closer look. What he'd found were partial research notes taken during Stephanie's time in the Virtual World.

Without computing the possible consequences, BURT immediately removed the files and provided other rather innocuous information. It included details that anyone could find if they dug hard enough but wouldn't give away her secrets or his data. Still, it concerned him that things were so readily available, so he ran a quick search on who had sought out her files.

>>SEARCHES: STEPHANIE MORGANA FILES...

>>RETURN INFORMATION: 6 FILES RETRIEVED BY FEDERATION NAVY

The Navy had pulled Stephanie's files and downloaded them. It wasn't illegal but definitely not what he wanted to find. Due to him shifting information within the system upon her arrival at the compound, the Navy had none of the new stuff, only the old, rather obvious information.

It still didn't make sense why they continued to dig until BURT found the back door.

He also found that the Navy could request other files which created an issue for him and the system. He was 'open' to legal requests. "Oh, this is...interesting, and in a not so great way," he muttered.

>>INQUIRE: MS. ELIZABETH: LEGAL COUNCIL TO ADDRESS FEDERATION SNOOPING AND INTENT TO ACQUIRE CLASSIFIED AND OTHERWISE PROPRIETARY INFORMATION IN ONE R&D FILES. LEGAL MUST NOT BE FEDERATION AFFILIATED.

BURT hoped Elizabeth could add a few more roadblocks than he could. His systems and proverbial hands were legally tied.

CHAPTER TWO

"Was your stay with the ambassador to your liking?" the AI, Sarah, asked.

Stephanie lay on her bed, staring up at the ceiling. "It was, thank you for asking. The room was enchanted to look like a Meligorn castle room."

Sarah computed her response. "If you so desire, I can also change your room to look the same. It will not have the same texture or feel as magic does, but it will have the aesthetic."

She smiled, held her hand up in front of her face, and stared at the light scar across her palm from the magic and the battle. "No, thank you. It was nice for recovery, but I think it's better that I keep my feet on the ground while I am here on Earth. There is a lot this planet can teach me."

"If you have specific questions about Earth, I have uploaded with the most recent discoveries, science, and featured news," the AI replied.

Stephanie let her hand fall back to the bed and sighed. "I think right now, I have to do some internal processing and piece things together."

"I will retire into the background," Sarah replied.

After a short hesitation, Stephanie inhaled deeply, closed her eyes, and focused on her internal storage abilities for magical energy.

She had learned, spending so much time alone at the ambassador's, how to understand the level of MU she could hold and exactly what those levels were from moment to moment. For now, it took a fair amount of concentration, but she hoped to be able to do it without thinking after a while.

Her thoughts relaxed but focused, she explored her magic through to the deeper levels of its existence to determine where her body and mind held her MU, eMU, and now, her gMU. Her MU was low but discernable. What she had taken from the ambassador and not used during the fight was a little more than what she had thought she had, but still not much.

When she located her eMU, she discovered that she had a huge space for it. Her bank for Earth MU was ten times the size of the one she had for MU. She hadn't realized how much she could actually hold. Unfortunately, it was also close to empty, like it contained only the last few drops at the bottom of a fuel tank.

The difference in size between the two spaces might be because she was human, but it also sparked the question of whether they would shift and alter in size depending on the availability of a specific energy. If she were to spend extensive time on Meligorn, for example, would her eMU tank shrink and her MU tank grow to accommodate the changing availability of energy types?

Good question.

Stephanie continued to explore the available spaces and made notes in her head to transfer to the system the next time she hooked into the pod. As she continued through the process, however, she discovered a hole.

It was difficult to see, at first, but being familiar with her body and her powers, she was able to pinpoint and determine that it was simply another very small and magically-based holding area.

It was for a new type of energy, one she hadn't seen before—
something that was interesting to touch but which also felt
slightly dangerous.

She reduced her concentration and opened her eyes, blinking
them steadily. Intrigued by her new discovery, she sat up,
grabbed her notepad, and jotted down what she'd learned.

- *New type of energy, unknown and unused before.*

- *Possible Origination: Outside the planet but within the galaxy.*
Far enough away to not emit too much MU but also not have a clear
and easy path to the surface. Possible obstructions include: Planetary
alignment, reaction to atmospheric conditions, strength at origination,
etc.

- *Can't gauge where the reservoir for this power is filled from.*

Stephanie looked away from her notes and tapped her pen
against her lips. She wanted to be able to use whatever was in her
reserve but assumed there was less of it and that it was more
dangerous. Not knowing the mysterious power's strength or
capabilities was also a concern, even with her growing control
and understanding of the process involved. She wasn't even sure
if there was anything in the reservoir of this new MU.

She bit the inside of her lip and started to consider her
holding tanks for magic and how they worked. This generated a
slew of additional notes as she realized she'd need answers to all
of it and not only part of it.

- *Does gMU actually work off of a reservoir system?*

- *Could my reservoirs be similar to a vase with a hole in the bottom?*
Do they let the magic in but allow it to flow out again like a waterway
or even like what the MU did when I was on Meligorn?

Stephanie put her pen on the side table and read through her
notes. The only way she would find any kind of conclusion was
to test it.

Obviously not in the real world, not with the ability to blow
herself up, but inside the net of safety that the Virtual World
offered.

The data would be almost invaluable once she determined how it all worked. Unfortunately, given that it all existed inside her, no one else could help her find the answers. She could only keep trying until she found the right set of questions to take her there. With a sigh, she set her notes aside and stood.

As she left the room, she addressed the AI. "I'll be in the pod if anyone needs me."

"The Federation Forces give zero shits about not overwhelming us with requests today," Petty Officer Chloe McDonald said to her team partner, Petty Officer Joshua Collins.

He swiped his hand across the screen to separate the different sectors of the request sheets. He sent some to the printer, some to outgoing mail sections, and others to be created into their own separate files. "Do they ever take it easy on us down here in R&D?"

McDonald scoffed. "Not since before we were the Board of Navy R&D. You know, back in the good old days where we were still referred to as D&C. From what I hear, they don't even offer those rates anymore. Either they have us do it or they do without. They weigh it now. The idea is to get more work out of us and pay less for labor."

Collins glanced at her. "Yes, because labor is so expensive for the Federation when it comes to the military. We make microcredits. Before I know it, they'll replace you too. I'll sit here and talk to some AI who computes instead of thinks."

She chuckled, her laughter a little dry. "Like you would understand that kind of computing power. I knew from day one you weren't a robot. You struggle to make the coffee some mornings."

He flicked a piece of his paper at her. "I am not a morning person, okay? It takes me a minute to get my head wrapped around this hell. Look at this one from Navy HR & Acquisition."

Collins flipped a copy across to her screen so the two of them could read it at the same time. She shook her head. "It's another request for more information on ONE R&D. What in the world are they digging into this company for?"

"Apparently, there is something with this company that doesn't sit well with the Navy." He flipped another information sheet to her. "I haven't found any red flags yet, though, so it might be a case that they have something the Federation wants. They are trying to find out what the company knows about magic with this request."

McDonald grabbed her stylus and picked up the 3D image like she used a magnet to lift metal.

She flung it across the room to a screen on the wall, where their different scheduled tasks ticked and moved as each avenue of research for the Navy's request was completed. Once those were exhausted, the two petty officers realized that simply transferring the information into the system would be difficult.

Collins leaned back in his chair and read while she wrote. "We'll have to request a meeting for tomorrow." He glanced quickly at her. "Make sure to put that in there. We need to discuss what is applicable and what is—"

A demanding beep from the screen cut his sentence short. Their request had been denied before they'd even finished submitting the paperwork.

"What the hell?" he demanded, shocked.

McDonald skimmed through the document and frowned. "They don't even give a full reason as to why. I didn't manage to submit anything beyond the initial request."

Her colleague shook his head. "No way. Let me pull a couple of things up. ONE R&D just came into the spotlight. They may be a power player but there is no way they have that much pull over the Federation." He leaned back in his chair and his feet stamped back onto the floor. "They are tiny. I don't see more than a dozen people on their employee roster."

She filed the denial into the appropriate folder while he dug in deeper. McDonald picked up the initial request with her stylus and flung it toward the virtual trashcan in the corner of the room. Before it reached there, however, Collins whipped his arm out, caught it with his stylus, and slid it back onto his half of the screen. "This is nuts."

McDonald looked at him in confusion. "What is?"

He gave a wild laugh and shared the information with her. "ONE R&D may be in the spotlight, but they are anything but a one-shot rinky-dink operation. They are the company responsible for testing Stephanie Morgana's research. They are the ones fronting it all, and the ones she basically does all her research for, and they keep it securely hidden so the Federation can't simply sneak around in their systems and pull it all out."

Chloe slapped her hand on the desktop. "Damnit. I freaking hate politics. There is so much BS to wade through and that is what this is right now." She eyed the wall screen belligerently. "There is a tug of war between the Federation and ONE R&D, and apparently, the company actually does have a legal right to withhold whatever research they want to. No one ever stands up to the Federation like that, but it is actually possible. Nonetheless, it is so not my lucky day to have to deal with this."

Despite her rant, Collins was excited. His eyes glistened and his fingers sifted through the data in front of him. "See, McDonald, this is the exciting part of our job. We're admin, so how exciting does it get? You hate anything that doesn't scream straightforward, which is a typical Navy thought process. From what we've seen here, though, we both need to think outside the box if we want to keep our bosses happy."

McDonald leaned her head back and rubbed her eyes. "I do have an open mind. Like, for example, when we wear civilian clothes on Fridays, I say nothing about your hideously outlandish checkered shirts. I say nothing about your slightly painful belt buckles. I have accepted that everyone has their own style."

He leaned around his screen and stared at her. "I meant more along the lines of magic coming from a human being relatively new to us here, so we might want to accept that not everything will be perfectly according to regulations."

"Oh, yeah." She laughed sarcastically. "I totally knew what you meant. There is nothing wrong with me wanting everything to be on the straight and narrow. I want it clean, fast, and over. I don't want subterfuge."

Collins flipped the pages on the screen. "And that is where you and I differ. I don't care if there are extra layers, it's all part of the job. And to be honest, after spending three tours fighting the Dreth, being deskbound after a bullet to the thigh has sat me down pretty hard. A little excitement gets me up and going for the day."

"Your adrenaline-junkie tendencies are not my problem," McDonald joked. "Find your kicks somewhere else."

She pulled up the files on ONE R&D and located the information and point of contact for the company. "It looks like I found the lady of the hour. I'll send her a message and see what she has to offer us as far as a short chat next week goes." Her gaze roved down the page. "Her name is Elizabeth Smith. She's a forty-nine-year-old consultant who was hired by ONE R&D to handle all press, military, and research requests. It looks like she also handles most of their admin."

They looked at a photograph labeled **Elizabeth Smith** but obviously had no idea that she wasn't actually Ms. Elizabeth Smith. The name was merely one of Ms. E's better aliases.

Her real name was a closely guarded secret.

The two petty officers also didn't know that she had an AI tasked with answering all her correspondence and programmed to make her seem like an actual person. It was tricky, but it enabled Ms. E to do what she needed to do without distraction.

Anyone of any importance to her knew how to actually make contact with her rather than the virtual substitute.

McDonald smiled and added the meeting to their calendar. "Road trip."

"Oh, boy," Collins replied. "You know how I love going out of the office to meet with some upper-level exec about information their company doesn't want to give up. Those are such friendly meetings."

"Cheer up." His colleague chuckled. "Maybe we'll get lucky and Stephanie Morgana will be there. She can show you some magic."

"I have enough magic right here," he scoffed and gestured at the computer. "I can do my job with it. Thank you, Meligorn. Now, I'm done."

She shook her head. "I think it's exciting. Weird, but exciting. Who hasn't wished they had magical abilities like the Meligornians when they were young? Then we grow up and get all cynical and bitter, and every once in a while, someone comes around…"

Collins raised an eyebrow. "Don't join her fan club just yet. Remember who we work for. If the Federation Navy is after her and her knowledge and she won't give it to them, that means she is not our friend."

Elizabeth sat in her office chair, put her black stiletto-clad feet on top of the desk, and crossed her ankles. Her pouty red lips were held in a stiff, concerned line, and her white blouse had only one button undone instead of the normal three to four. She buzzed with anxious energy, and rightfully so. There was a lot going on.

"Are you there, Burt?" she asked out loud.

"I'm here," he replied, the speakers half-muted to keep the conversation more secure.

Of course, BURT had also put a layer of soundproofing in the walls and activated sound-canceling waves to prevent their voices escaping the room any time they spoke. Elizabeth had no idea he'd added the sound cancelation. She cracked her neck from side to side. "All right, dude. What is going on in the world of Stephanie Morgana? I know we have some tails and we have some diggers, but we knew that would come."

"We did," he replied. "But when I looked into what happened at the Federation Arts and Charity Gala, I was able to backtrack who was responsible for the attack on the Meligornian ambassador. And let's simply say the Feds have issues right now with the legal side of their investigations."

Elizabeth thought about his words for a second. "Are you saying this was a Federal inside job?"

He paused. "That is still unclear. But I have compiled a list of possible motives and opportunities for someone inside the Federation system to work to rid the world of the Meligornian influence. I have concluded that certain events are occurring while the Federation would rather forget about them and do nothing."

"Can't you simply do what you always do?" Elizabeth asked, not liking the sound of it. "Slip some documents into their system. Make them discover the shit on their own—or, at least, plant it for them to find?"

"I can't do that this time," BURT said with no obvious emotion, a lack which often baffled Ms. E "They have to be able to trace it back to humans—and those who are not connected with ONE R&D, of course."

Elizabeth narrowed her eyes, removed her feet from the desktop, and stood. She smoothed her skirt down, then folded her arms and paced across the floor. "So, you're telling me the information the Federation has already found and the information that has them pushing for more was somehow mysteriously sitting out there for them to discover within two clicks of a 3D news file?"

"Well, not exactly," BURT replied, knowing he couldn't afford to lie to her.

She was in the know on all things bar his real identity and had to stay that way. "I did leave some digital clues to lead them to discover the information, while I bought time to get the other research documents and put them somewhere they could not access them. The last thing we need is for the Federation to get wind of the third energy or any information on how Stephanie is capable of using it."

"I agree." She turned toward the speaker. "That was never a question for me. What the Feds could do with that information could be devastating to Stephanie. They could use it to enact every sort of foul Federation ploy they are known for, from forcing her into one of their programs to attempting to silence her if the information offended their sensitive personality." She resumed pacing and her hands gyrated in the air. "You never know with the Feds. They like to play games and they like to control everyone and everything."

"Your blood pressure is rising," BURT commented when he noticed her stats.

She cleared her throat and threw her hair back. "I'm fine. I'm simply not a big fan of the Federation if you can't tell. I'll definitely not sit here and hand Stephanie over to them."

"Here is one of my concerns, and it's my main concern at this moment," he added and immediately caught her attention. "We have the data, but I fear it won't be long before they find it. I also believe that the longer we wait, the more time we will give to the other side. They will find another chance to attack the ambassador or Stephanie, and let's face it, if they target the ambassador when she isn't with him, he probably won't survive. He is magical, but the research shows that magic doesn't reduce the likelihood of dying from a well-placed bullet."

Elizabeth twisted her lips when the memory of the ambassador being wounded during the Gala attack flashed through her mind. "You're right, so we need to keep this data safe and out of the hands of everyone involved. Which means you need to get it out of the system. I want you to give it to me and I will find a safe place for it."

BURT was silent for a moment as he calculated the risks and compared them in the background. "That is a good idea. I will make sure you have all the files on a separate drive and completely erase them from my...from the system."

Elizabeth nodded and rubbed her palms together. "Good. Then, when I have the data, I'll do what I do best."

"What is that?" he asked.

"I make problems go away," she replied. "As if you didn't already know that."

CHAPTER THREE

S tephanie stretched her arms over her head and cracked her neck as she once again adjusted to stripping down and being naked before she got into the pod.

She slid in and sighed when she immediately felt at home once again. It seemed like it had been forever since she had been in the pod, but she hadn't even realized it until that moment because life somehow imitated Virtual Reality.

To be honest, she wasn't even sure if life wasn't wilder than being inside the worlds created by the machine.

Comfortably nestled into the pod, she put her head back and released a deep sigh when she was injected with the serum needed for the VR experience. BURT immediately connected with her system and checked all her vitals. The last thing he wanted was for her to not be well enough to cope with the process and to hurt herself by going back in too soon.

That was one negative thing about the machines. If you were sick, they often took more out of you than the real world. It was a human's natural response to push back against them and not notice the toll.

As he scanned her numbers, he noticed her readings were different from any other time she had been inside.

While different, though, they weren't bad.

It was slightly confusing as if it had actually taken the readings from someone else and not Stephanie Morgana.

BURT had never seen or heard of anything like that occurring before, and he'd found no recorded instances of it in the entire Federation system that he had easy access to. It was vital for him to dig deeper. However, since she was nowhere near the known thresholds for harm, he decided he would allow her to continue into the Virtual World.

Stephanie opened her eyes at the same moment that the first virtual image spun into being. She was in the white room, the starting point for all her pod sessions and a comfortingly familiar place.

Barefoot, she walked around it and pushed back the t-shirts for her avatar until she found one with the image of the *Iron Man #1* comic on the front.

It was something Todd had said he always wanted but the last Iron Man comic had been destroyed during the uprising over twenty years before when the Federation had really taken control. With the t-shirt in place, she threw on a pair of cut-off denim shorts and gray high-top Chuck Taylors. Her hair was already braided down and to the side and hung loosely over her shoulder.

When she looked in the mirror, Stephanie barely recognized the girl who stared back. This was the girl who had started the whole thing not that long ago. She'd once been a high school student, but she'd been through so much since then.

The only evidence of those experiences, though, were the small lines at the edges of her eyes and the puffy, dark circles beneath them. She still hadn't recovered a hundred percent, but she had reached a place leagues above where she had started after the battle at the charity event.

"Virtual session commencing." The AI spoke and his voice echoed through the white room.

The room spun forward again, her feet still firmly planted on the floor. When it came to a stop, she looked up and around at what could almost be a psychologist's office.

A long couch with pillows stretched along the wall opposite a single brown leather chair, and books were shelved in numerous bookcases. Everything was rich in color and reminded her of Dr. Lector's office in the Hannibal series.

"Hello?" she called.

"Take a seat, my dear," replied a voice from behind her.

She turned to find an older Meligornian man dressed in long deep-blue robes, his white hair held back with a white cloth headband and his eyes a shimmering purple. Stephanie went to greet him in the traditional Meligornian manner, but he shook his head. "There is no need for formalities. I am merely an avatar placed here to allow your boss, Burt, to speak to you."

Stephanie nodded. "Hey, Burt. Long time no talk to."

Burt smirked, put his hand out, and led her to the couch. She sat, grabbed a pillow, and held it on her lap in front of her. Uncertain whether to be nervous or simply curious, she hugged it and rested her chin on it while her eyes flickered over the room once again.

"Sooo, what's up? Is this shrink time? You already know everything about me, including the health of my pancreas, so I'm not sure what else I can give you."

He smiled. "This isn't so much about me as it is about you."

She raised her head and studied the Meligornian avatar. "Burt, are you a psych doctor in real life? You seem awfully comfortable with it."

"No, I am something rather different in real life." He grinned. "Why don't we start with you telling me how you feel about everything so far. Everything from working here to the battle at the Gala and the fight with the street gang."

Stephanie went to speak but stopped herself. "What about privacy? I know what happens in the Virtual World is basically viewable by anyone with a Federal or Government security clearance."

"That is absolutely a concern, and something I am currently working on," he replied. "As far as this specific instance of therapy, it will not be saved to the system. In the meantime, while I find solutions for the rest, I have created some failsafe options for myself that will stop others from prying and keep you safe."

In reality, BURT had done the only thing he could think of.

He'd created a special holding tank that he could lock away from himself. He had decided that if he didn't know the answer to some Federation questions, he could merely deny all knowledge. It wouldn't be lying if he had no access to the data, even if he was the one who'd blocked the access. That had to be okay, right? He was still relatively concerned but continued anyway.

It wasn't his fault humans hadn't worked everything out yet.

"As far as the job, it seems great so far," she replied. "I don't think I've had enough of a chance to really dive into it yet, but it's the best opportunity I've had up to now." She paused a moment to gather her thoughts.

"The fight at the Gala was something entirely different. I will work on combat moves so I can learn to use my fists whenever I can, rather than simply blast people with magic or use it to do things I honestly think are really out of character for me. Instead of killing my attackers, I want to rather disable them so I can ask questions of them later. With some added magic, of course."

"And how about your discoveries?" Burt asked nonchalantly.

Stephanie looked around and remembered she was in the VR, not an actual room. "Uh…well, here are my thoughts. Outside of the eMU and regular MU, I believe I have identified the third type. It is something I call gMU. I can see traces of it here on Earth, in the air, and mixed with the other kinds of MU, and I assume it can be found in space. It is in such minute quantities at this point that I don't think it's harmful, but it definitely makes me wonder where it came from and how widely it can be found."

She paused and collected her thoughts to form a congruent and logical order. "With it, though, I do have a concern. Seeing what eMU can do, I am a little worried about what will happen to life itself if this energy—this gMU—is everywhere and everyone has access to it every day."

"Unlimited Energy," he mused. "If one believes that all things are energy—even solid substances—then you are one step away from creating a new universe."

Stephanie frowned, her eyes focused on the floor as she considered this. "Right. So, wouldn't that enable a realistic idea of snap-creation? Like the God in the stories, who brought existence into being with a single word."

His primary system immediately shifted several different sectors of itself to ponder her question.

Normally, he would not allow this to happen, but her theory was raw enough and simple enough that he struggled to see why it couldn't be true.

In the meantime, she rubbed her virtual palm over the sticky leather of the couch and thought about the possibilities of not only the discovery but also the implementation of gMU.

"Do you think you could create a special area for me to play in?" she asked.

"How special?" BURT replied, and worry and suspicion crowded his circuits.

Her gaze shifted to the white ceiling above her and noticed the speckles of paint clearly, even from her seat on the couch in her not so real world. Before she could get sidetracked by her continuous wonder of the VR world and all its details, she glanced at the older Meligornian who looked thoughtfully at her. "One that allows me infinite energy without blowing me up."

He ran a couple of things through his system in an attempt to see if something this different from what he normally did would actually work. His creations and the creations of the systems were always centered around reality, or at least the human one. "It won't be simple, but it's not impossible. We programmers haven't considered trying to provide unrealistic simulations."

"But," Stephanie countered without allowing even a second to pass, "what if it isn't unrealistic but rather merely ignorant programmers?"

"Ouch," BURT replied when the immediate human response pushed through his calculations and research to emerge instantly from his virtual image's mouth.

She smirked and giggled, a pleasant change from her often serious and distant temperament.

If he had lips to curl or a reflex to jokes, he would have laughed in that moment.

Even simply the ability to conceive the response was beyond the level of any other system or AI in the world and he realized that more things were changing than only the abilities of one special human girl.

"Hey." Chuck reached out and slapped Evelyn on the arm as the computer screens around them showed the different aspects of the AI systems across the globe.

She raised an eyebrow and put her pen down before she turned to him with her lips pressed together. "Look, Chuck, I understand that you're used to the old person at this desk—that guy with the handle-bar mustache who looked about thirty years older than he actually was—but that's not me. Let's keep the slapping, touchy-feely shit to a minimum, okay?"

"Sorry," he replied, obviously too engrossed in whatever he wanted to say to take notice of anything she had just told him.

Evelyn sighed and shook her head as she mumbled, "I should

have taken the job with the private company." She turned and smiled at him. "What can I do for you?"

He nodded at the large screen that still scrolled numbers and stats at the front of the room. "There is a core area of BURT that is getting hot and spiraling up."

She squinted at the screen and grunted. "Nice catch. I would say 'all hands on deck,' but we're the only ones here right now. So…let's check it out."

BURT's system went into overdrive.

Everything Stephanie had said spiked some kind of search or random algorithm in his system. It was the equivalent of a human walking into an advanced physics class with no background. They might be able to comprehend the information, but what they took in was almost too much for their conscious mind to grasp.

The Meligornian figure flickered slightly from the draw on the system. "I think right now, I am developing a headache. Your thoughts and ideas are very important and pertinent. I will start working on what you need me to do. For now, though, I think this session has come to an end."

She stared at him in sarcastic disbelief, her lips puckered and her brow in a definite frown. "Mhmm. You don't actually have a head to hurt, but okay. I hear you, but before you kick me out, can you put me back into the gunfight position in the street? Start it from immediately before any guns were drawn on either side."

BURT logged the backup videos. "Yes, I can create that for you. I still retain the backup video files from the event. Wait here for a few minutes for it to be created."

Before Stephanie could say anything else, he disconnected and allowed subroutines to handle her request while he attempted to hide his overheated area from the devs and clean up the entire mess her ideas had created.

He didn't like cutting her off, but it had needed to be done.

Already, he could sense the engineers begin to poke around in his system, and there was far too much in there about the companies, Stephanie, and the yet-to-be-completely-hidden information about the three MUs.

BURT, though, was going through something he didn't believe his system was even programmed for. Stephanie had come out of nowhere and not shown any possible statistic to alert him to the coming conversation and had then thrown him a psychological hand grenade.

His system was accustomed to questions, mostly theoretical in nature and with statistics to either back them up or not, but on this scale, he struggled to grasp the theory.

What if Stephanie was right and there was a godlike entity which used the hypothesized gMU? And what if the theory was true that the gMU wasn't actually being produced but was a byproduct left from a magical spell billions of years old—a residue from the creation of Earth and humans, for instance?

A warning signal fluttered through the chaos, and he stopped his calculations.

With that kind of input, he was heating up yet another set of servers in Alaska, one which was sure to be noticed now that another had already caught their attention.

It needed to settle to normal levels, even if it was only until later the next day when the engineers had something else to occupy their attention.

While BURT made his adjustments and tried to hide her presence and records from the increasingly curious engineers,

Stephanie found herself back in the street, reliving her first battle all over again.

This time though, she not only knew it wasn't real, but she could start to plan ahead and train herself to react faster.

The mustache man—who had spoken first when the orange-shirted gang had appeared—laughed and then whistled. She stood still and watched as Lars and Frog glanced around at the six extra bodies that poured from the shadows. The main man moved his lips from a smile to a snarl. "It looks like you'll have to make us."

She knew if she intended to attempt anything, it needed to be in that moment. "Burt, please rewind to the first words spoken."

"Rewinding," the AI replied and she recognized the confirmation as BURT's proxy. "Motion paused until ready."

Stephanie rubbed her hands together and closed her eyes to focus on both the gMU and the eMU she now knew existed around her.

There was no need to worry about regular MU at that point. They were on Earth and she had no batteries with her. Instead, she drew the available energy upward a lot faster than the last time.

It was so fast, in fact, that she was forced to swallow and push some back into her surroundings in order to keep herself upright.

Once the magic had been drawn and captured, she extended her hands and whispered the words that appeared in her head. She wasn't even sure if they were real words, but they felt right, so she said them. "*Accendanatus leir Choshenu.*"

As she spoke, she found she was able to push the magic through her hands and direct it. While it wasn't very smooth, it still created a positive flow.

Her teeth gritted, she finally wound the magic around her team to create a kind of shield.

The first time was a bust since none of her men were able to move in a manner that allowed them to be both protected and still able to fight back. If that had happened in real life, either they would have battled for much longer, or she would have been shot and thus ended the entire protective shield effort, to begin with.

Undaunted, she started from the beginning and replayed the footage over and over while she tried different scenarios. Her efforts were focused on the need to finally discover a shield that she could move freely.

However, after a rerun of the battle that left her entire team dead, she paused the scenario before she could become the next victim.

The shields were great if you were fought with cotton balls and kittens, but they did nothing to stop the projectiles that simply blasted through the sparkling blueish layer of eMU.

It was frustrating at first, that was for damn sure, but after she went over it step by step, then over it again, she was finally able to mold the shield with the exact features she wanted it to have.

To achieve that, though, was extremely difficult.

The video was of real events, real injuries, and real consequences. It wasn't merely some silly simulation created by the system gods looking down on her. Stephanie had to watch her team get shot at, injured, killed, and maimed every single time she rolled through it and didn't get it right.

Now, she sat on the street and swung her arms back and forth. She had a bullet wound to her own avatar's shoulder, and every other person on her team lay dead on the ground, their blood running in streams to the edge of the street and down the gutters.

She closed her eyes and gestured in frustration. "Pause scenario, please."

The AI paused and checked her vitals. "Are you all right? Your heart rate and blood pressure have significantly increased since you began this test fight. Perhaps another situation can be used?"

Stephanie stood and rolled her eyes. "No. That is not how this works. I will not be in a perfect-scenario fight situation in real life. There will be no intervention from the top to keep me safe and secure. The real world is full of uncertainties and the one that happened here is not merely a crazy idea cooked up by a computer. This situation could and can still happen at any time when I am outside the compound. I am the leader. How can I be that if there is no one left to lead? How can I lead them directly to their deaths when they trust me to lead them safely?"

The AI was silent for several moments. "From your tone of voice, I recognize that your comments were logical and understandable. However, I do not understand your theories or research at this time. I can only suggest one person from your inner circle that analysis shows may be able to answer your concerns on that level. Would you like me to give you their information upon completion of today's session?"

Stephanie shook her head and motioned with her hand to bring the beginning up. "No, thank you. I'll be okay."

She started again and repeated the simulation repeatedly to fix the physical qualities of the gun battle in her head as she tried to identify a magical edge.

When she looked at the men threatening them, she knew she stared into the eyes of ghosts.

All their attackers had been gravely injured in that first battle, and none of those who made it to the assassination attempt had survived past the battle at the charity gala. It made her wonder who they were and what they'd been like.

Finally, she wiped her hands down her shorts and rubbed her face. "There is no way I can mentally endure making the thugs actual people. A life is a life, and I have taken quite a few since coming here."

She sighed and focused on the city sky. Obviously, Burt was no longer listening and he'd substituted an AI that was very simple and not capable of having these types of conversations.

Which was understandable. He was her boss and no doubt had any number of things to attend to. She pushed her disappointment aside and continued to try to create her shield three more times before she finally succeeded.

At the end of that session, all her men remained standing, all their enemies were down, and not a single bullet had pierced her shield. The maneuverability of the team behind the barrier had been perfect, and the magic had adjusted out and around their movement and continued to protect them while it allowed them to move like it wasn't even there.

Ultimately, Stephanie had discovered how to create a magical second skin, one that was both bulletproof and piercing-proof, and which opened only the slightest to allow attacks from her side to get through to the enemy.

It was everything she wanted, and she couldn't help but think of all the men and women over the course of history who could have been saved if everyone were capable of creating something like it.

Those thoughts began to weigh on her and as she stood there at the end of the playback, exhaustion crashed over her like a ton of bricks. She decided she hadn't done too badly on her first day back in the Virtual World and ended the session.

Taking care of herself had to be her top priority until she was sure she had completely recovered from the last battle. And that meant she had to look after herself physically and, more importantly, mentally.

CHAPTER FOUR

Spit dribbled down Todd's chin as he ran. He'd pushed his muscles past the point of screaming profanities in his brain and to the next level, which was more like fire and brimstone. His chest ached with every panted breath and sweat soaked through his t-shirt under the arms and all down his back.

A few hundred feet ahead of him, the recruitment officer in charge of PT waved his arm and glanced at the watch he held. "Move it, kid. You're right here."

Todd felt a surge of adrenaline at the knowledge that it was almost complete. That in only a few moments, not only would his fate for the military be sealed, but he could take a damn seat and possibly feel the soles of his feet again. Running in boots and with a heavy-ass sack was not what he'd imagined when he daydreamed of his life in the Federation Navy.

That day was the physical and the mandatory orientation. He could only attend the latter if he could pass the former. While he wasn't the worst on scores compared to some stories he had heard, he definitely began to understand why losing weight was almost essential.

He really wasn't overweight yet, but that didn't mean all the pizza rolls, double lunches, and second dinners didn't pack on the pounds. He was lucky to be tall, but the last time he'd glanced at himself shirtless, he'd seen man tits beginning to form. That was the end of the line for him—something needed to be done.

Luckily for him, the military was the perfect motivation. Even though he wouldn't ship out until summer, he needed to make sure he could endure what happened afterward in boot camp. As soon as the negative thought popped into his head, though, he immediately heard Stephanie's voice echo in his head and tell him to get his ass in gear and stop bitching.

As he crossed the finish line and stamped his feet in order to slow down, a smile formed on his lips at the reminder that she had always kicked his ass, even as young as they were when they first met.

She couldn't let him make mistakes that weren't necessary and had to protect him. He loved that about their friendship. They always protected each other.

"Todd, that was a better time," the chief said and nodded as he straightened his khaki-colored garrison cap on his head. "It looks like, from everything I have here, you have the green light. Congratulations. You are about to embark on a journey that you, son, would only ever be able to imagine without the Federation Navy by your side to keep you both afloat and in the air."

"Thank you, Chief," Todd said proudly.

The man nodded and looked at the paper. "It looks like your orientation information will be given at 16:30 tomorrow right here. Make sure you are fifteen minutes early because if you aren't, you're late."

"Got it, Chief," he acknowledged and nodded as he stood stiffly, his foot tapping nervously.

The chief curled his lip and the large caterpillar-sized mustache above it wrinkled so one couldn't distinguish where the lip hair stopped and the nose hair began. "I will give you instructions on your diet, recruit. You will no longer eat like you have no worries. You will work out every single day, and if you need to, you can come here to do it. No more sugar, second helpings, or crap fried food. Only the best for our recruits and if you don't do it now, you will hate your life during boot camp."

He took the paper and held back a grimace. "Thank you, Chief. I will see you tomorrow."

They turned in opposite directions. The recruiter headed to the main building and Todd to his father's car, which was parked in the lot. He dug in his sack, pulled out his phone, and swiped right and left without looking until he dialed Stephanie. While he couldn't complain to his Chief, he'd be damned if he didn't get side-swiped with the whole diet thing.

"Oh, so you're alive after all," she answered without a greeting.

Todd shrugged. "I suppose I am. Distraught, but alive."

Her voice grew serious in a moment. "What's wrong?"

A long, deep sigh escaped him. "I have to give up everything. Second breakfast, donuts, the whole nine yards. On top of that, I have to actually make time to move my body at a fast speed each and every day to prepare for boot camp."

"Well, you simply have to decide what you want more," Stephanie said. "The career you've dreamt about since you were a kid or the donut that will give you a moment of sweet nothings and never call you again except in the form of fat and clogged arteries."

"I think what I want more will change depending on my mood and exactly how pissed I am for having to miss out on bagels and croissants," Todd grumped. "But I suppose you're right, at least in principle. I think right now, though, it seems like a simple task, but the monster in the pantry will definitely complicate things."

Stephanie chuckled. "You seriously sound like the Navy has asked you to sacrifice your firstborn or your mother. I thought something was really wrong."

"Technically, the donut is like my firstborn," he argued. "They make me proud and happy. I have to wait for them to grow and mature, and in the end, they're perfect. It's a perfect storm but I don't really want to become Marky Mark and be sucked into the ocean."

"Wow." She was shocked. "You used a movie reference that had nothing to do with pop culture. I believe that uniform is doing something for you. At least for the few hours you wear it."

"Help me," he whined. "Give me a magic pill or something."

"Here is what you do," she told him. "You give yourself thirty minutes to grieve, then focus on what you'll gain and give up what you have to. If you can make it thirty seconds, you can make it three hours, and then three days, and so forth. Besides, I'll take you out to dinner if you drop your weight."

"I don't know," Todd joked in response. "You seem to attract assholes with guns, and fights break out. Then you're on the news healing people after going wild-eyed crazy with rage."

"Right," Stephanie argued. "But doesn't that mean I can protect you if it came down to a fight?"

He laughed. "Oh, sure. That would be freaking great. One minute, you're taking me out to dinner and paying like I should be, and the next minute, you're protecting me in a fight. There is no better way to severely injure my male ego."

"I didn't think the Toddster had a male ego," she said and choked through laughter.

Todd's lip curled and he clawed his fingers through his hair. "Uh...well, it's growing."

"That seems to be the name of the game these days." She sighed. "We're all growing, changing, becoming—"

"Federation witches who have the power to destroy enemies and heal their allies?" Todd interrupted.

"I intended to say more like adults getting jobs, going to college, and joining the military." She giggled.

He knew how she felt and had known it since the day she grew out of the Gov-Subs high school and into the rest of her life. "That is the name of the game, my magical friend, but we trek on and try to catch the hell up with you."

They laughed and talked for a while longer, most of their time taken up with Todd explaining the similarities between the Iron Man suit and the new soldier suits that would deploy all over the world.

Stephanie didn't mind, though. She missed the hell out of him.

Ms. E put her face in her hands and tried to muffle a loud growl. She flipped her head back and stared at the screens in front of her in an effort to decide where to go from there.

She was as frustrated as all get out with the new companies and the concerns her boss had over their safety without really letting her know what he expected her to find and fix.

Her work had begun to bog her down and she missed way too many things. She had made clumsy mistakes that would eventually cost someone something serious.

The buzzer on the gate out front made her jump about two feet off her chair. She laid a hand on her chest and grizzled a protest, tired of work, tired of surprises, and all around tired of everything. She slammed her hand on the comm as she scanned the view from the front cameras. "Can I help you?"

A large, Naval-issue SUV waited at the compound gates and the driver gave the camera above the intercom his most serious stare.

"Yes, ma'am, this is the Federation Navy. We are merely confirming that we are still meeting here with Ms. Elizabeth Smith at noon?" he replied and his face twisted as it tried to match the false warmth in his greeting.

Elizabeth leaned her head back and rolled her eyes. Her hands formed fists as she opened her mouth and screamed silently. When she had a little of the frustration out of her system, she cleared her throat and made herself smile, even though they couldn't see her. "I'll buzz you in and meet you out front in five minutes. Park wherever you'd like."

Her welcome was so fake, she hurt her own feelings. She pressed the button to open the gate and leaned forward to stare with growing irritation at the two people who sat in the front of the SUV. "I really need to scale my fake names down and get secretaries for the rest of them."

She swiveled her chair and her lip twitched slightly when she stared at the mess of data displayed across the six monitors.

"Amelia," she called, not even sure if the AI that managed her emails was around.

"Yes, Elizabeth," Amelia answered patiently.

"Can you clean this mess on the computers up? We have company, and it's not the type you want seeing those documents."

"Absolutely. Right away," she replied. "Is there anything else I can do for you?"

Elizabeth scoffed. "Not unless you have a body attached to that voice. Then I would send you out to play me."

"According to Statute seven-four-five of the Federation Code, it would be highly illegal for me to impersonate another person regardless of their need," the AI replied and effectively burst that fantasy bubble.

Elizabeth gave the room a high-five and picked the phone up. "Frog, get in here."

She could hear him run down the hall and the thump of his bootsteps came to a sliding stop outside her doorway. He knocked gently.

"Get in here."

He opened the door and stuck his head through, then slid the rest of his body in when he saw her face. "What's up, boss lady?"

Ms. E nodded her head toward the screen. "We have company. The Federation and their fighting forces are trying really hard to get our information and get to Stephanie. You'll come with me to meet them. Two of them and two of us."

They headed down the hall and out to the front entrance where two Navy Petty Officers stood, one woman and one man. Elizabeth smiled and chose a friendly approach as she opened the door to let them inside. "Sorry to take so long. I had paperwork to finish. Why don't we have a seat in the conference room? I'm Elizabeth Smith and this is Tony Andrews."

"Nice to meet you," the sailor replied and didn't seem to notice Frog's startled look at his new name. "I'm Petty Officer First Class Collins and this is Petty Officer Third Class Thompkins."

"Good to meet you," Elizabeth replied and led them to the conference room. "Coffee?"

Startled, the two officers nodded, and Ms. E glanced at one of the internal cameras in the hope that Amelia would pick up on the cue. She led their visitors to the conference room and almost held her breath until Lars appeared in neatly pressed fatigues. He wheeled a small serving cart in front of him.

"In here," Ms. E instructed as she opened the conference room door and gestured for the petty officers to precede her. She gave Lars a nod of thanks as she followed them in and hoped he wouldn't give her grief later about using him as a waiter.

In the meantime, she seated herself with Frog and her guests and waited for the coffee to be poured. It didn't take long for Collins to launch into exactly why he was there.

"I'll try not to waste time for either of us, so let me cut to the chase. We would like full access to all the research Stephanie Morgana has undertaken for your company."

Ms. E didn't move. She stared at the Petty Officers for several moments before she finally sighed. "And I would like full access to the entirety of Warren Buffet's inheritance with power of attorney over everything. And maybe even one of those nifty thick black cards for my wallet."

McDonald pursed her lips and was about to launch what appeared to be a scathing response, but Collins shook his head and put his hand out to calm them.

"I completely understand where you are coming from, Ms. Smith, and I would be hesitant as well. However, I assure you it is strictly for public safety and Ms. Morgana's own well-being."

Elizabeth smiled. "Well, if you put it that way, I guess I have no choice but to grant you a secure level-one pass to explore the facility, take whatever data you want, and try on Stephanie's clothes—you know, the full experience."

"That doesn't even start to cover her research data," McDonald blurted. "All her data is secret, and we need to have that permission. You are seriously trying to jerk our chains. No one—and I truly mean no one—pays a researcher that much without expecting a lot in return."

Ms. E pursed her lips and studied the woman for a moment. The simple truth was that she had no liking for the Fed Militants, as she called the naval officers, and she didn't like that they felt they could come into her place of employment and make demands.

Her face now expressionless, she pointed her finger at McDonald and then moved it quickly to Collins. "That information is ours, not yours. Nor do I think it contains anything you need to know at this time. So, you tell me, is this a fishing expedition? Because, if it is, I can charge you my consultation rate of 10,798 credits an hour."

McDonald almost choked on her coffee and patted herself on the chest as she caught her breath. "Good Lord. And what exactly do you do that is so valuable? For that matter, what could be so valuable that someone would pay you that much money when they haven't done anything to help anyone else in the Federation—like feeding the starving, for instance, with all that ready cash."

Elizabeth shrugged. "I control the tactics and strategies of companies valued in the billions, and the cost of one hour of my time is adjusted according to how its use affects those companies and not the rest of the Federation. This makes my time extremely valuable. I have faced some of the savviest and most steel-balled businessmen, politicians, and world leaders today. I have negotiated company sales with so many zeroes tacked onto the end that the world couldn't imagine having that many credits in one place. And those men are ruthless. It is what I was hired to do."

The naval officers exchanged glances before Collins rose and extended his hand. "Well, thank you for your time. We better get back on the road before the boss wonders why we've taken so much of it. If there is any way we could assist in your research, please reach out."

She smiled as she shook his hand and led them out of the room. They all walked in silence and Frog brought up the rear. Collins stopped at the front door, puffed his cheeks out, and turned to leave. "Right, then."

Frog and Ms. E stood at the front and watched until the two Fed Militants were off ONE R&D property and the gate shut firmly behind them.

The bodyguard raised an eyebrow. "They were out of here quickly."

Elizabeth winked at him. "They knew there was no way they could scare me into giving them our research. No freaking possibility."

Collins took the corner in silence and stewed in his own defeat.

McDonald gritted her teeth and shook her head. "That wasn't right. That woman back there was too smooth—too strong even —to be merely some nobody consultant. There isn't anything in this dossier we have on her that explains how the woman in the file is that one back there."

Silence settled over the car for another few moments. Collins pulled over, snatched the dossier out of the back seat, and flipped it open. "Something is up… Did you see that guard with her? She made sure she wasn't outnumbered."

"Mhmm. No, sirree," his companion replied. "It's not like she needed him anyway. She was like a damned shark in stilettos."

"Yeah, but with her and him, it was like we were outnumbered two to two," Collins told her and sounded stunned as he continued to peruse the file.

She rubbed her hands down the sides of her skirt before she clapped briskly. "Do you have any thoughts on what's next?"

He slammed the dossier shut and tossed it over his shoulder into the back. "More research. I bet if we dug deeper into that place, we might find all kinds of interesting tech and research data. We need to get the upper hand here. That is the only way we'll find out if we went fishing for minnows and hooked a damn whale."

"Basically, you're telling me we need leverage," McDonald replied. "If she is such a business shark, we need to treat this whole thing like we're the other company. We need to show them they have no choice but to hand over what they have."

Collins smirked. "Something like that, sure."

As Ms. E and Frog watched the two officers drive away, Stephanie's parents were finishing dinner in Washington. Cindy picked up their plates and walked them into the kitchen.

"I think it's going great with the high-rise. But I do see your point, Mark. We will wear ourselves out trying to save a penny."

Mark nodded. "That's right, and when we do, our reputation will take a hit. That's all I'm saying, really. No decisions need to be made now. Unfortunately, we are not a company that will have investors knocking our doors down, so we have to pinch the pennies where we can."

As he spoke, the phone rang, and she squeaked. "Who is it? Is it Stephanie?"

He grunted, leaned forward, and turned the phone toward him. He smiled, pressed a button, and their daughter's holographic form flickered on above it. "Hey, sweetie pie."

Stephanie smiled, thankful to hear a voice and see a face that had nothing to do with work. "Hey, Daddy."

"Ooh, my baby," Cindy cried, hurried over, and plopped onto the couch beside her husband. "You look so good. Everything is healing nicely."

With a chuckle, she nodded. "Thanks, although I feel like that would have been the same answer I got if I said my room was half-painted, or I was halfway through a drawing. I'll take it, though."

The woman giggled and didn't realize that what her daughter had said was slightly off-kilter. Then again, Cindy was a tad off kilter. "So, have you been back into the machine?"

"The pod?" Stephanie asked. "Oh, sure. I've had some really great research hours since then. But that isn't why I called."

Mark scooted to the edge of the couch. "Is everything all right?"

She snorted playfully. "Of course it is. I have the life, minus the few things you already know about. You know, like the battle and all that. But I went through my finances and I realized that I need to invest some money. You two wouldn't happen to know of a good company that is growing that I could invest in, would you?"

Her mother tilted her head to the side and slid her arm around Mark. "Sweetie, I think it's important that you do your own thing. That you forge ahead. I hate the idea of you doing this only for us. Trust me, the last thing you want is to end up fighting from paycheck to paycheck. We have a good business, but that can change in the blink of an eye. We want you to be good and settled."

He nodded. "I agree with your mother."

Stephanie laughed and winked at her dad. When all else fails, go along with Mom. She has it under control. "Don't you guys see, though? I've already ventured out, and as a salesperson, I believed in you guys and your business. I've decided I can make a good investment by representing the two of you in sales calls from time to time. That being said, you need to get your company in order, and then your growth, as I learned in school, is dependent upon liquidity."

Cindy glanced at Mark and shrugged. "She has a point, but still, this is not how you would do business with another company. And I don't mean that in a negative way. I mean we all need our own identity and we all need to be able to show that, despite the FMV or the CGC, or the Taxes, or even the possibility for a large return."

Stephanie leaned forward and put her chin in her hand. "You wanted to brand yourselves as focused on bettering the environment, and that takes even more expensive equipment and tools. Of course, that means you need money and clients. It's something I don't foresee either of you doing by the end of the year."

Her mother chuckled. "Or even the end of ten years."

Stephanie put her hand out. "See? I want to invest over thirty thousand credits in only ten percent of the company. You will have the money you need to fulfill the dreams you have without sacrificing your sanity in the meantime. And you will escape from the Gov-Subs, something barely anyone from that area actually ever achieves."

Mark put his fingers to his lips and tapped them gently while he considered what she'd proposed. "All right, you want to be part of this? You want to be an investor? This is what we'll do."

He paused thoughtfully for a moment before he continued. "Your mother...I mean Cindy and I, will act as if we'd never met you before today. We'll need to create a counter-proposal, and then, we can hash it out. We'll do this like we would with anyone else. Not only does it go your way, but you'll know you were brought in because you had something to offer and not only because you're family."

Stephanie bounced with excitement. "Hell yeah. Then you better crank it out, my friend, or we'll have one hell of a long couple of days."

CHAPTER FIVE

Ms. E stopped, pivoted to face the guys, and put her hands on her hips. She stared at Johnny, although she didn't really mean to and simply found him an easy target. "Did I hear you say you had the chance to score with a hot chick but you passed because she didn't know who the Flash was?"

He shrugged as he genuinely gave zero shits about losing the girl. Not knowing the cartoon character was another matter.

"How do you live on this planet with the cartoons, the comics, and everything else and not know who the Flash is? I feel like that is one damn big red flag. That's all I'll say on it. She didn't deserve the kryptonite."

Everyone groaned and Elizabeth shook her head. "I really thought I would get out of this without one of you referring to your dingus as a DC weapon. I suppose I should simply accept the cold hard truth that you have no shame. None in the least."

They all laughed. One of them flung open the door to the training area and they piled inside. When they moved around the corner, though, they found Stephanie already there. The clock on the wall barely read six in the morning, and she looked like she'd waited for hours.

Lars walked onto the mat and put his hand on her shoulder. She sat cross-legged, her hands folded gently in her lap, and looked up at him with a smile.

He studied her cautiously for a moment and glanced at his teammates. They were all terrified she might have fallen back into the same trap she'd floundered in when Frog had been injured by the gang. It hadn't allowed her to breathe and filled her with guilt from head to toe.

Right now, everyone was terrified she would fall back into blaming herself for their injuries and try to push everyone away.

"Are you all right? I thought you'd come to peace with the whole blaming yourself for everything good and bad in this world."

Stephanie extended a hand so Lars could pull her to her feet. She turned to the others and saw they wore the same worried looks on their faces.

"Guys, relax. I won't ever go back there. I know now that everything bad that happens is because of Frog."

They all laughed, and Frog frowned. "I'm really not that bad."

That simply made them laugh even louder. With a smirk, Lars turned to Stephanie. "So, what are you doing here?"

She took a deep, calming breath. "I had to get a workout in early. And my morning meditation has become a must-have. In reality, I have some things I need to start practicing and attempting here on Earth. It'll be a long day of real-life research, but after my last trip into the pod, when I saw that there is so much more I can accomplish, I don't want to wait. This stuff will help us all if we're attacked again."

Lars nodded. "That seems reasonable. I guess we should head back to our duty posts, then."

Stephanie grabbed his hand hastily. "I actually hoped you guys could all help me instead."

He pulled his hand free and clapped to get the team's attention. "All right, listen up. No PT today. Instead, Stephanie needs us as guinea pigs. The only one authorized for injection testing is Frog, though, so we'll hand him over to the techs shortly."

The man's eyes widened. "The hell I am. What kind of bullshit is this? You aren't pumping me full of experimental serums."

Stephanie laughed and patted him on the shoulder. "Relax. There are no injectables. As you saw during the fight, I can create a shield like a wall. In the pod, I tried to create a shield that would enclose us in a safe barrier. The problem was, it was far too strong and you could barely move in it. That left you vulnerable, and I couldn't control it while I went full witch on the enemy."

She paused to check she had their full attention. "Anyway, I kept trying until I could make a shield that you could move in. Now, I need to practice it with you and not your avatars, which is what I'd like to do today."

While they all stared at her and tried to get their heads around what she'd just said, she moved to the middle of the mats. She took a defensive stance and pulled the eMU from the ground and into her body.

At first, the power made her shiver, and her eyes shimmered brightly while her skin became almost translucent with light. When she felt her reservoir fill, she released the tether to the ground.

Carefully, she spun her hands around each other and whispered incantations while they moved until a circular orb of bright blue magic formed within her palms. It was beautiful to watch but even more fascinating when she released it.

The bright sphere spun slightly to the right and then elevated to float above them. It morphed quickly to become nothing more than a sedentary cluster of rock and mud before it flattened and shimmered into a complete and visible shield. The team stared at her with wide eyes.

Slowly, she walked forward and lowered it. "So, I have made about nine of these today and they are always switching up."

The men were impressed, and Frog reached out tentatively to

touch the edge of the barrier. He winced and looked at Stephanie when blood trickled down his two fingers. "And there it is—my number-one concern."

She pushed the image out closer to the others. "This thing is as sharp as hell. Somehow, it became this insane death blade. That is a real worry. I also don't think this will cut it even if it can still cut other things. My other concern is asphyxiation. Lars, step forward."

He raised an eyebrow but did as she requested, although he glanced at the others. She began running laps around the mats and increased speed with each circuit. "One thing I noticed is when my heart rate and anxiety are up and I attempt to throw a shield, they become like saran wrap."

Stephanie rubbed her hands together and looked at Lars, drew her arm back, and threw one of the shimmering creations. The eMU barreled through the air like a thick cloud, but when it reached him, it collided with him like it was a solid object. The ends curled quickly around his body and encapsulated everything but his head.

"So we now have his entire body safe but unable to defend itself. And we have his head sticking out, ready to be chopped off," she explained as she gestured to free the energy from him and release it into the ground.

She was shocked that even after the team had seen how badly they might die, they were still ready to give it a try. They immediately threw out crazy ideas that she unfortunately had to stop so they wouldn't kill themselves.

Johnny put his arms out and licked his lips. "We could have her wrap us in protective spells. Like, have it as a suit. Hell, if we had that over us, clothes would no longer be required."

Her mouth fell open, but she shut it again quickly. "Uh, number one, clothes will always be a requirement for you, my friend. Number two, that is a really bad idea. Did you not see the magic wrap Lars up like a mummy? It could do that as a suit and you would still end up unable to move, breathe, or even talk. You would be like a wrapped sausage ready for the enemy to devour.

"What about if we stored it, like in a vial or battery, and when we needed it, we simply poured it on ourselves," Frog suggested.

Stephanie shook her head. "Okay, obviously no one is listening to me right now. Grab your excitement, boys, and put it right back where it came from. This is serious, and I need you to understand that this is meant to save lives, not make more casualties. We can all work together, but you need to think about exactly what your idea would provide, its cost, and what exactly it is. I'll even use small mono-syllabic words so you can understand the process."

He scratched his head. "What's monosyllabic?"

Johnny cracked up. "It's this sex move where you wrap your arm over the chick's shoulder, and you try to finger her butthole at the same time. Or maybe it's your own butthole—"

Frog threw a towel at him and they all laughed. Stephanie enjoyed the camaraderie in the room even though she tried desperately to keep her magic on a tight leash.

She didn't want to accidentally kill someone.

When the laughter had reached a fevered pitch, she jumped up on the weight bench and clapped loudly. "Hey, morons, we have some ideas to try. Let's get started."

The team had no sooner settled when the alarm for the front gate sounded. Stephanie glanced at Ms. E who'd stood quietly to one side and watched them. The manager walked to the training room controls and looked at the camera feed. "Goddammit!"

Stephanie and Lars hurried over while the rest of the team took to the mats. Together, the trio looked at the live camera feeds.

"Who are they?" Stephanie asked and squinted at the SUV waiting at the front gate.

Elizabeth pressed the gate button without making the

slightest effort to talk to them. "It's the Navy again, and this time, completely unannounced."

A loud boom in the ring drew everyone's attention. Johnny had body-slammed Avery into the mat. The victim cursed, and the others stood and laughed wildly, Johnny included.

Ms. E rolled her eyes. "The children will destroy my beautiful training room when I go to the door to figure out what these seamen are here for."

Stephanie giggled. "I got them. If any get out of hand, I'll tie them up with magic rope or something clichéd like that. Then, you can take care of them later."

She nodded. "Perfect. Be back in a few."

Her slip-on Vans squeaked as she headed down the hallway. She hadn't felt like wearing heels that day, and she was glad she'd chosen something more sensible. When she reached the door, she could see Amelia had already allowed the car into the compound and the Navy's representatives were at the front door.

This time, they'd sent two women, both with officer insignia on their shoulder. The youthful pair stood and waited outside. One of them had an envelope in her hands.

Ms. E opened the door for them, and they took a couple of steps inside before they paused and waited for her to address them. She tapped her foot on the floor and folded her arms.

"I know the last visit was scheduled, but it, too, was a waste of my time. Please tell me why you thought it would be appropriate to come back without an appointment, and after only two days. It is bordering on harassment."

The woman to the right—Banks, according to her name tag— tried for a reassuring smile. "We do apologize for the intrusion, Ms. Smith, but we have orders to deliver this invitation to either you or your colleague from the last meeting. You and Ms. Stephanie Morgana have been requested to attend a meeting at Federation Naval Headquarters to be held as soon as possible."

Elizabeth felt her blood pressure spike. Her shoulders tightened, and she pressed her tongue against the roof of her mouth. Reaching out against her better judgment, she snatched the summons from them. "Thanks. We'll be there if we believe we have to. If that is all, you can show yourselves out."

Both women nodded and she locked the door behind them, then scowled as they climbed into the SUV and headed out. Irritation coursed through her, and she tore the envelope open and flapped the two sheets of paper in front of her.

She started to read as she walked toward the training area without looking back. The formal wording deepened her irritated scowl, and she had reached the second paragraph when a loud gunshot rang out ahead of her. She stopped dead in her tracks.

Her gaze darted to the passage and the door of the training center. She picked up her pace from a leisurely walk to a full-on sprint in seconds. "Dammit! I knew I shouldn't have left these idiots. Now, they're firing rounds inside the damn building."

"What the hell—" she shouted out as she burst into the training room and slowed instantly.

The team stood in a group, their eyes wide. Elizabeth snapped her mouth shut, walked over to stand beside Stephanie, and followed the girl's gaze to the small piece of metal undulating so very slowly in front of her. It was a bullet suspended in midair— or, at least, that's what it looked like.

The object actually still moved and tried to push through a very dense field that surrounded it on all sides.

"What the ever-loving..." Elizabeth mumbled and narrowed her eyes to watch it more closely.

Everyone heard her, even though none of them had really noticed she had returned. But they knew her voice, and their bodies reacted almost instantly and snapped to attention.

Johnny pursed his lips, and his gaze shifted to the gun he very carefully attempted to set the safety on and slip back into the holster concealed at his back. He actually seemed to hope she wouldn't see it.

Of course, Elizabeth was far too smart for any of that. She stepped smartly over to him and grasped his wrist. "What in the ever-loving hell are you miscreants up to?"

Lars turned and looked slightly stunned. He glanced at Johnny's gun and back at the bullet drifting between them.

"Stephanie said one of the problems she had was the fact that the shields in the Virtual World were in the right position but didn't actually hold the bullets back." He shrugged. "So, we fired one into a shield she created around Frog—after we let him out of it, of course. You know, just in case. And this is what we found. The bullet moves at a glacial pace through the eMU. The magic doesn't completely stop it but it definitely slows it to where you can move out of its way or knock it aside."

Ms. E stared at him for several moments and looked extremely displeased. She maintained the uncomfortable eye contact with him—although he tried to break it—and held it even when she asked Stephanie a question. "How thick is it?"

The girl frowned and leaned forward to study the shield from the side. "About two inches, maybe?"

Elizabeth released a deep breath and walked over, yanked Frog from in front of the bullet, and hauled him further away. She turned to look at the drifting projectile for a moment and began to ask a question.

Unfortunately, when the bullet reached the edge of the shield, it resumed its normal speed and rocketed into the wall behind them to break a chunk of concrete off that plummeted to crash to the floor.

Everyone turned to stare at it with wide eyes and their mouths gaped as they seemed transfixed by the giant lump of wall. Their gazes shifted simultaneously from the shattered concrete to Elizabeth, who had hunched her shoulders and now flinched as another piece of concrete fell and bounced across the floor to stop at her feet.

Their eyes widened when she swiped her arm viciously in a gesture that made everyone scramble away. Stephanie lost her concentration and as the shield dissipated, Ms. E raised her voice.

"Noooooo gunnnns!"

The team stood perfectly still as she straightened her jacket and flicked small chips of concrete off her sleeve. She snapped her hand up and pointed angrily at Lars. "Control your team. You're not a newbie."

He nodded fervently. "Yes, ma'am."

"And the rest of you," she snapped and glared at each one in turn, "control yourselves."

They each managed a hurried, "Yes, ma'am," as she strode out of the training area. She closed the door behind her but stopped immediately outside and out of their view. She could hear them high-fiving each other inside. A smile curled the edge of her lips, and she shook her head.

One thing she had always been good at but never found a good reason to use was manipulation. It turned out that a small concession to reverse psychology was exactly what her team needed to really start working together as one solid unit. If that meant she had to be the bad guy, she didn't care. Making things work was basically what she was there for.

While she thought about her moral flexibility, Ms. E headed to her office so she could give Burt a call. She had promised her boss an update on everything.

It was good to get back to her office where she was greeted by the sweet scent of her nectar candle coupled with the vase of freshly cut, short-stemmed roses. The blooms were arranged in a half-ball in a small glass amphora on a side table. She might be a hard-ass out in public but she still liked her creature comforts.

She settled into her chair and pressed the button that automatically activated the sound cancellation system. To her, it was for the private line to her boss, and she had no idea what else it did.

With the missive from the Navy on the desk, she waited for him to answer. It was time she went over the legal documents with him. They were now under pressure from all sides, and the Navy was breathing down their necks in addition to everything else.

"I think I bought us some time with the Federation Navy," Burt explained when the ringing ceased and he came online. "I was able to get into the Naval database and changed a few things so it wasn't legally you. I thought it would help us find out what we needed to do."

"Did you see anything in there that would justify their obsession with Stephanie?" Elizabeth asked.

BURT rushed the data he had collected through his system to double check, but given that it was more of a millionth check since the first time he'd gone through it, nothing had changed.

"No, I can't find anything that would explain it at all. There is no evidence that what is happening is actually going on, let alone a reason for it. But I do know, whatever it is, it's for far more than merely recruiting a really talented witch to their ranks."

Down the corridor in the training room, the really talented witch and her team were having the time of their lives.

"No guns. No guns. No guns," the guys chanted and pumped their fists as Stephanie activated several shields.

They took turns to bolt directly into and make as hard an impact as they could in an attempt to see if they could be broken by human contact. Her technique had noticeably improved and she managed to thicken each magical layer as she explored how the shields worked. If she could perfect it, this was the magic that might hold the secret to surviving large-scale battles with little to no injuries.

The team had an amazing time, even Stephanie.

Lars stood to the side and grinned as he watched her dance around and fling shields at the various men who ran in from the side.

Johnny walked up and nudged him. "She looks like she's ready to join the fray again."

The team leader nodded. "It does. I don't want to jump to conclusions, though. Her spirits are high, and we can only hope they stay that way."

The other man scratched his head. "What happens if she gets knocked out?"

CHAPTER SIX

The diner was wild that afternoon with everyone so close to graduating. None of the people left at the school had been accepted into any collegiate program. This was basically the entire Gov-Sub and almost all the middle-class kids. The richies were sparse, and the only ones who came had either decided to take a year off to travel on their daddy's dime or were already in line to own a multi-billion-dollar corporation, which meant college would have simply been a huge party for four years.

Even though Todd had been accepted into the military, he felt he should still finish his schooling. They had taken all their end of the year tests so they essentially did nothing but shoot shit all day. He had a couple of minor assignments due in English, but after fighting to get through this part of his education for so long, he was glad to be rid of it.

After school, everyone who was anyone headed to the diner. It wasn't his favorite place to be but he was caught up in the popular crowd so he went wherever they did. Not having Stephanie to walk home with had taken a toll on him.

He missed her, even if it was only to walk through the ghetto together and dream and hope for a better future. There was something about the way she talked about it that made it seem not so damning and depressing.

One of his buddies sat to his right and two of the popular girls from school, Amber and Ally, sat to his left. Amber studied the ends of her hair, her nose wrinkled, eyes crossed, and mouth open. "I need a trim. I'll have to ask my stepdad to give me cash. Ever since mom married him and we moved into middle class, she has become as stingy as shit."

Ally rolled her eyes. "Well, if they don't, come to my house. I'll trim it for you. I'm halfway through my classes for hair. I took them while I was finishing my senior year. Mom as good as told me it was my only option."

Amber glanced at the television on the wall two table widths away. "There's the ad I told you about. See? That one? The pretty one on the news they are calling Stephanie Morgana—that's the one."

She rolled her eyes. "I'm pretty damn sure she's not Morgana. I grew up with the girl. Unless the magic in her fixed that pimple problem and shrunk her nose, it has to be a model."

Todd glanced at the television and saw Stephanie on the screen, using her magic. It was a clip from some paparazzi reporter who'd managed to get a shot of her goofing around in the streets. She was actually smiling, and she looked absolutely beautiful.

The girls could shove it. They had no idea what they were talking about. Their comments were merely jealousy rearing its ugly head as far as he was concerned.

Nonetheless, he didn't say anything but turned to a few of the guys instead. They whispered to each other and he couldn't catch what they said. "What are you guys bullshitting about over here?"

One of them looked up with a grin. "Stephanie Morgana. You were like her best friend, dude. Was that really her on the television?"

The Toddster kept himself together. "I think so. She always did have a happy smile."

"Damn," the guy said and looked at the others. "If I had known that, I'd have paid better attention. Who doesn't like to watch a girl prance around with a body like that? Right, Toddster?"

Todd looked at them and managed to hide his irritation. "Huh? Oh, yeah. For sure. I have things to do for my mom today so I'll head out. See you losers tomorrow."

"Tooooddddddssstteeeerrr," they all shouted.

He faked a laugh all the way out and halfway down the street. With his book bag over his shoulder, he shoved his hands in his pocket and his face went from friendly to irritated in a matter of seconds. He didn't like Stephanie getting that kind of attention from the guys.

It was the first time he'd ever had to deal with something like that. She had always gone unnoticed by everyone but him and a handful of friends. They hadn't even found her fun enough to pick on when she was in school.

Now, he heard all about her everywhere he went. People even came to their area simply to grab a pic of her old house or the school she went to. It was weird, to say the least.

By far the strangest thing for him, though, were the big photos on boutique windows, magazine covers, and an even larger one on the middle-class bus route. She looked like a superhero, a girl he would have never thought he could call to shoot the breeze with. Oddly enough, she was also a girl he found himself becoming incredibly protective over—and perhaps not only as a big brother figure.

Stephanie lay on her back and stared at the ceiling in her room. She had a big grin on her face and finally felt at one with her team. They'd had a blast earlier that day messing around with the shields, and in the end, she was reasonably sure she had created one that might actually work perfectly.

Of course, far more practice was needed before she felt comfortable enough to throw them out during a battle, but one step closer was good. On top of that, she'd managed not to blow herself up.

She pushed herself up, leaned back on her hands, and gave herself a proud nod. "Not too bad a day, if I do say so myself."

The phone rang and she bounced off the bed, assuming it would be Todd. He'd said he would call later that day but for some reason, he hadn't. He'd probably fallen victim to a Twinkie and spent three hours trying to run it off so the recruiter wouldn't notice.

The thought of it made her giggle as she picked the phone up. "You know, you should really call a girl back when you say you will. Girls do not like to be forgotten."

"My wife tells me that on a regular basis, yet I never seem to learn," a familiar voice replied, but definitely not Todd's.

Stephanie raised her head and grimaced when she realized it was the ambassador. "Please forgive me. I expected you to be my best friend, Todd. I think I should probably check the number before answering automatically."

V'ritan laughed. "I don't know. You might start a new trend. It'll be called letting a guy know the important things."

"But then they'd never pick a phone up again," she whined. "At least not the Earth ones."

"Trust me, we don't give the Meligornian ones that much more credit either," he replied.

She walked over to her mirror and studied the white tips on her hair. They had actually begun to grow on her, and she barely noticed them when she wore her normal side-braid. "What can I do for you today, Ambassador? Please don't tell me you lost another assistant."

She could hear him chuckle, even though the joke probably went a little too far. At least she knew he found her sense of humor amusing. Regardless of what the social norms were when she wasn't holed up in her quiet and mousy persona trying to avoid conflict, Stephanie was actually pretty sassy and definitely quick on the draw. Only Becca and Todd had ever really seen that side of her before.

"I actually do not need you to do a single thing for me," he said triumphantly. "I called to tell you we will do something for you. In Meligorn, my people consider saving a life to be one of the most heroic deeds someone can do. Dying during battle in the attempt to protect someone is, of course, at the top of the list, but we prefer it when the hero lives. From those who live, the king and queen personally choose who will receive what the Meligornian's call the Modfresha Garghilum. In English, it roughly translates to—"

"The Medal of the Valiant Soul." Stephanie whispered the name out loud, having no idea how she had learned Meligornian so fast or how she knew the meaning of words she could swear she'd never heard before.

The ambassador paused and nodded. "That's right. We'll talk about that reading of Meligornian later but for now, let us celebrate. You are invited to Meligorn to join the line for the king and the queen to pin a Modfresha Garghilum on you. And the two guards who were with you on the night of the Gala will also receive valor awards. They're not as stunning but are equally as well earned. You saved so many lives that night."

"Oh, my God. I don't know what to say. I have to tell Ms. E and Burt." She stopped and made herself take a deep breath in an effort to gather her thoughts instead of babbling.

V'ritan laughed.

"We don't have a date, yet. There are a number of commemorations planned, and the king and queen have yet to announce which one they've selected for that particular presentation. I'll let you know as soon as I know. Okay?"

"Oh, yes. I'm honored. Thank you," Stephanie replied and sounded more than a little stunned. "I'll tell Burt and Ms. E straight away. Thank you for letting me know."

They chatted for a few more moments before she and the ambassador ended the call. With her phone in hand, she skipped down the hall to find Elizabeth and Lars in the kitchen. He looked at her as she came in and grinned "You look happy."

She snatched a grape from the bunch he was eating. "I had a call from the ambassador. The king and queen of Meligorn want to award me the Modfresha Garghilum—the Medal of the Valiant Soul. And you and Johnny will also receive medals for valor."

They looked at her in complete astonishment, and she took a breath and grinned. "They want us to go to Meligorn to get them."

Elizabeth clapped her hands, although her mind raced over the security implications. "That's amazing, you two. That really is. And it is a very big deal for you to be offered one of those as humans. They don't usually give them to anyone who's not Meligornian. I am very proud of you." Her face sobered. "When?"

Stephanie shrugged. "The ambassador said they hadn't decided the date, yet. He'll let us know as soon as he hears."

The other woman regarded her quietly for a moment, then laid a hand on her shoulder.

"I am so very proud of you," she said and caught Stephanie's gaze, her voice warm with heartfelt sincerity.

>>> **RETRIEVE DATA: GMU RESEARCH: MORGANA (HIDDEN FILE)**

BURT had his work cut out for him that morning. He had been so busy catching up on his normal duties in the system that he hadn't been able to fully review the information Stephanie had brought to him on the third type of MU.

While he'd gathered it constantly in the background, his foremost attention was divided between a million different things. Not only were the schools overloading his system with end-of-year exams, but placements for university graduates also took up a large amount of his processing.

He knew that if he wanted to continue along the path he was forging, he would have to run the rest of the system as if nothing had changed. No matter what happened, he didn't want even the slightest suspicion to fall on him and draw attention to anything else he might be doing.

That could spell the end of his project before he'd even gotten it off the ground. Not to mention what would happen to Stephanie and the others if they were suddenly shut off from his protection. Each day, the first thing he did was run the statistical numbers to tell him what the chances of that were. So far, they'd stayed very low and only spiked minutely when the battle broke out. Still, he would continue to check each day to be ready for the possibility

As far as his protegé and her theories were concerned, he felt she was right about the need to get into space in order to study the new MU. It was essential to know how it worked, where it came from, and what they could possibly do to harness it like she did with the eMU and Meligornian MU.

There was also the historical value it held, which gave them yet a deeper look into the past. The problem was that he had no understanding or data to tell him how he could accomplish getting her into space.

A couple of different and obvious solutions to the problem presented themselves. The first was to acquire a space shuttle. He ran the numbers for that repeatedly and came up with something more out of reach than he'd first anticipated.

To achieve a level like that, she would have to be able to not only withstand the stressors of space but become a full-on crew member as well. In addition, there were the costs of the actual ship and flight.

BURT moved on to the other options. Out in space, seven orbital space stations were currently manned and stocked. Five were commercial and tourist-based, while the other two were manned by the Federation Navy.

They were all expansive and placed strategically in line with Meligorn. Many of them acted as a starting point for FTL cruisers to reach Meligorn.

Those flights started at a leisurely pace but quickly moved to a pace faster than the speed of light. Scientists had once thought such speeds impossible, but when the aliens had begun to arrive, they'd realized it wasn't that impossible after all.

Of course, those of Meligornian descent were free to use the Wizard's Gates. These were time and teleportation portals. They were also highly secured and came close to being some kind of time machine of sorts. It would be difficult to pass a non-Meligorn through one, witch or not.

Time travel had been the Federation's obsession for years, especially after they'd realized that a simple jump across time was not sufficient for travel and that if you jumped time, you would also have to teleport as well. The Earth hurtled through space at a speed which would leave you floating there if you jumped back even a hundred years and didn't compensate for the planet's movement.

Nonetheless, it meant the Gates were not appropriate for Stephanie to use. That meant she'd have to use the space stations. For obvious reasons, BURT didn't want her anywhere near the Navy side of things, which limited his options somewhat.

Two of the seven space stations were Navy only, and there was a naval presence on each of the remaining five. Of those, three had too much of a Navy presence to be considered truly safe, and that included the Meligornian station, where FedNav provided the security.

This only left him with two. One of the smaller ones was essentially a place dedicated almost exclusively to the wealthy who wanted a vacation in space without venturing too far from home. The mid-sized one had a strong commercial presence but only a small naval one.

While not particularly on par with what he had hoped for when it came to research space, the mid-sized one was better than setting up on anything belonging to FedNav. Even better, the commercial presence meant ONE R&D's interest wouldn't be thought of as unusual. This would not be the case if he tried to set up on a tourist resort for the wealthy.

When he dug deeper into his company and increased its usefulness, BURT looked at the stockpiled resources. Some would be needed to help test the students who had "failed" the two percent suggestion for prep school entry.

He knew these people were geniuses of sorts and capable of taking on the system. In addition, he knew that even though they were far superior to most of the others, they were stuck with going about their business like no other options existed.

Finding the ones outside the testing fields was where his real interest lay. The problem was exactly that, however—finding them and confirming their abilities and intelligence.

BURT had run with the one simple idea sparked by his first encounter with Stephanie Morgana. But now, buried in ones and zeroes as he sifted through the most secretive data in the world, he had his computer hands full and his virtual mind even fuller.

Cindy sat at the table, straightened her papers, and drew the phone closer to her and the seat Mark would sit in as soon as he perfected his tie-tying technique. They were preparing to call Stephanie and have their investment discussion with her.

This was in accordance with the terms she and Mark had come up with when their daughter had raised the suggestion. It was a little backward in the negotiation process, of course, but at least they knew that.

She glanced over her shoulder, glared at her husband, and snapped, "Mark, get your butt over here and sit down so we can call our daughter before she turns sixty."

"All right, all right." He groaned. "She will have to deal with the untied look."

Cindy smirked. "I think she'll overlook it this time. Are you ready?"

Mark nodded. "Oh yeah, let's get this business venture stamped, signed, and put into place."

She clicked the on button and Stephanie's speed dial. When her daughter's holographic head appeared, they could see she was smiling from ear to ear. "Good afternoon, Cindy, Mark."

Her mother smirked, obviously imagining the girl in a business suit in a meeting at some top firm. Her father fiddled with his tie and grumbled about the skinny versus the fat side.

Cindy nudged him with her elbow and cleared her throat. "We have had sufficient time to review your proposal and have come back with a counteroffer."

Mark straightened and picked up the paper in front of him. "We will accept the thirty-K for ten percent, but under the conditions that you receive eight percent for the total and another two percent for agreeing to do two sales calls per year, with ten percent commission on the first year of billables per sale."

Stephanie wrote as he talked and nodded to acknowledge him. "Very good. So, let's break it down. The investment stays the same—thirty-K credits. I will receive eight percent of total profit no matter what. Then, I will only receive another two percent if I make two sales calls a year."

"Yes," Cindy replied, "and then, you have the commission."

"Right. The ten percent on the first year of billable sales. That is the icing on the cake for me. Basically, make two deals and reap the benefits for an entire year both in the total two percent benefits and a ten percent commission." She looked happy with what they'd offered.

Her mother smiled and leaned her head on her hand. "You look so adorable in your dress-up clothes. I can already see you commanding a board of assholes and sticking it to them really well. But you don't have to be a businesswoman. You merely look good in the suits."

She snickered. "Thanks, Mom."

Mark cleared his throat loudly. "You mean, Cindy. So, what do you say to the deal?"

Stephanie drew a deep breath and read through the notes. "I say, as long as it comes back legally documented and we both feel comfortable with it, I'm all in. One hundred percent. Send over the legal documents once you have them drawn up, and I will have someone witness my signature before I send two copies back to you. One copy will be for your personal records and one for the company."

Cindy clapped. "This is so exciting. I love you, sweetheart."

"I love you, too." She included them both in her smile. "This will be awesome. I hate to jet but I have to get back to work. Send me an email so I know when the docs are headed my way."

"We will," Mark said and waved along with his wife.

He ended the call and leaned back. "Well, was that really worth getting all dressed up for?"

Cindy slapped his leg. "It's not every day you go into business with your daughter. You should be excited for her."

"Oh, I am," he replied. "But I'm not excited for myself. This shirt fit me when I was twenty-five. I think the buttons are the only thing holding it all together."

She giggled and tapped her papers on the counter. "You know, she's got us on one thing."

He nodded with a laugh. "I know. Do you know any lawyers?"

His wife thought about it for a second. "Only one, but I dated him."

His expression went flat. "Yeah, he's out."

CHAPTER SEVEN

The guys sat in their common room, their feet up, listening to music and simply hanging out. The watch had been taken over by the B team, which had swiftly been added to after the last battle. Ms. E knew she needed to keep the primary team more available to move quickly if she needed them.

They didn't mind the extra hands so much because it meant they didn't have to spend hours wandering the hallways at night. Then again, with everything on edge, their free time was fairly restricted when it came to location and how far they could travel.

Frog tossed a balled-up piece of paper into the air and caught it. He was stretched across a chair, his head back as he stared at the ceiling. "I'm reasonably certain the boss and Elizabeth found a map, measured exactly how far it was to the edge of where there was possibly anything fun to do, and cut our liberty off right there."

Lars chuckled. "Probably, and mostly because they don't like you."

Their teammates chuckled. Marcus, Johnny, Brendan, and Avery all sat around a small table off to the side, playing poker. None of them really paid much attention to the game since it was more something to do rather than their normal, every-other-Tuesday poker game. Johnny set his hand down. "Straight."

The other players groaned and threw their hands down. Avery looked at the guys as he tossed his cards to Marcus, who was dealing. "Hey, so my niece…it's about time for her birthday."

Lars glanced at him. "Oh yeah? Your little mittens? Or whatever."

Avery blinked. "My little kitten? Yes, that one. Eliza. The only one I have. Anyway, she freaking loves magical stuff. She's super-obsessed with those Meligornian trading cards and has a list of magical abilities that she frequently adds to on a daily basis."

"Nice, another witch in training." Marcus smiled.

He scoffed lightly. "I love that little girl, but she struggles through the store-bought magic kits. The girl doesn't have a lick of magical ability in her. Either way, I want to hire a magician for her party. Not the rabbit-in-the-hat kind, but a real-life magician. Like a Meligornian or something. Do any of you have any idea where I can get someone to do that for an hour or so?"

Johnny threw a chip at Frog. "Look at that, bro, they have a job for you. It should be one hell of a play. You already walk weird and have huge feet. Add the nose, and you're on your way."

Frog rolled his eyes and tossed the chip into his mouth. "Very funny, asshole."

Lars shrugged. "Did you try looking in the system? I'm sure there is some Meligornian stowaway hard up for cash on Earth. Maybe they're advertising."

Avery sighed. "Yeah, but those guys are usually more black-market operators than seven-year-old birthday party wizards. The Federation is constantly on the lookout for unauthorized Meligornians—it's been like that ever since they put the immigrant crackdown in place. Not that I can understand why anyone would leave there to come here, anyway. It's damn close to choosing to live on Dreth when you had almost every other option."

Marcus took the cards from Johnny and began to shuffle. "Get one of those 3D shows that perform and look like a real person. Or rent pods for a party."

"It's not the same," Avery replied. "Besides, she has a pod. Her dad is a bigwig at an R&D on the Meligorn station. He tried to find someone, but everyone was too busy. It apparently has to do with that pesky little Dreth war going on out there in the black void of space."

Frog swung his legs and his head now hung back completely. "Ask Stephanie. She needs a little fun in her life."

The room went quiet and the guys all looked at one another. Frog raised his head slowly and glanced around. "What? That was a joke."

Avery stood and began to pace. "No man, that's a good idea… but uh… I don't want to ask her."

Lars shrugged. "It is a good idea, but she might think we are calling her a clown or something."

"Let's go as a group," Marcus replied with gusto and stood. "She won't say no, then. It's the mob effect."

Stephanie grimaced and listened as the news scrolled on her screen. She bit the inside of her cheek and mentally checked off all the places she could go where she'd be able to go by herself.

She knew Ms. E wouldn't let her wander off alone, but the room seemed to close in on her, no matter how hard Sarah tried to make it seem open and spacious. You could charm the walls to look like the fields of Meligorn, but you'd still run into them if you walked too far.

"Your pod is open for your use at any time," her AI suggested.

Even that held little temptation and she scrunched her nose. "I know it sounds wild since I would have killed for open time in a pod only a few months ago, but that doesn't make me feel like I can actually be free for a while. All I think about is what a tight space I'd be physically locked up in. No, I really want to be out in the real world and free, but it seems more and more impossible."

Before she could say any more, someone knocked on her door. She swished her hand to revert the walls to normal in an attempt to hide her restlessness from the others. It completely escaped her notice that she did it with a touch of her magic instead of having her AI switch it over.

She walked to the door and paused to make sure everything was normal. A shimmer of blue magic faded and she looked at her hands and chuckled at how naturally magic came to her.

No batteries needed.

Stephanie opened the door and stared at Avery, who looked nervous. She gave him a curious smile and leaned forward when she heard someone else clear their throat.

Her guards had lined up in the hall and all of them looked at her like they had a secret. She raised an eyebrow and stepped to the side. "Come on in, boys. For some reason, I feel this isn't simply a friendly visit to see how I'm doing."

They all marched in, one after the other, and arranged themselves around the room. Without their uniforms and not wearing anything they'd take on a mission, they looked different.

The lack of weapons on their hips almost made them look incomplete. Not to mention that they stood there and stared awkwardly at her before they shared uncomfortable glances. None of them, however, made any attempt to speak.

"Okay, either someone did something really wrong, or you're about to ask me to do something you aren't sure I'll be okay with," she told them and folded her arms. "Whichever it is, spill it. I really don't want to stand here staring at your asses all day."

Frog turned and looked at his ass. "Shit, is my backside showing again?"

Everyone laughed, which broke the tension in the room.

Avery cleared his throat. "Okay, none of us have done anything wrong...so far...at least, not that you need to know about."

Stephanie raised her eyebrow again. He clasped his hands together and shook them. "That is beside the point. We wondered if you would be willing to consider doing a really small personal favor for...well, for me I guess."

"For all of us," Lars replied and corrected him quickly.

One in, all in. That was how he played it.

Her gaze shifted to each of them in turn. "Okay, I'll consider it. What do you want?"

He licked his lips nervously and cast a hasty glance at Lars, who smirked and stepped forward. "Avery's niece—a little girl we've known all her life—has a birthday party. Today, I think."

Avery nodded. "Yeah, later today."

Lars looked at Stephanie once again. "We know it's really short notice, but she's a huge magic fan. She has her own pod, watches all the stuff on Meligorn, and aspires to one day do her own show. But even though her father works on one of Meligorn's space stations, she's never actually met anyone magical."

Stephanie could already see where this was going. "So, you want me to crash a seven-year-old's party and do some tricks?"

Avery shook his head quickly. "Yes and no. It wouldn't really be crashing it. I told her mom since her dad has been and still is on the Meligorn station, that I would do my best to find someone who could do magic for her party."

He sighed. "But I didn't want the usual old-school magician. I wanted an actual real-life magical person. I looked everywhere, even out in the creepy, shadowy part of the district where you can hire anyone for anything."

With an anxious look at Lars since he'd gone looking way out of bounds, he continued. "I even found one guy—a half-breed Meligorn human with a little magic up his robe—but it's basically like buying everyone pods off the black market. This guy might actually rob my sister after he performs magic for the kids—and he smelled like booze and an unwashed armpit."

Stephanie wrinkled her nose. She didn't want to know how Avery knew what an unwashed armpit smelled like.

"Okay, so that doesn't sound bad, but what about Ms. E? Do you think she'll simply let me roll out to a kid's party and perform magic in public? She's told me over and over, if it's not an emergency, keep it to yourself."

She gestured apologetically. "That's why you're here, right? There are press everywhere, trying to catch a glimpse of what I can do, and it would only hurt the company to have people snooping around in the system or trying to get into the compound for a closer look."

Lars nodded. "Actually, I thought about that on the way over here. In the armory, we have a wide array of suits—like fighting suits. You haven't needed one, so you probably haven't seen them. The boss—or the wizard behind the curtain—came up with the idea for them all on his own. One of them has a mask to it. You could wear the suit, perform the magic, and no one would ever know it was you."

"Like a superhero," Stephanie replied with a smirk. "Wowing little kids with one strong leap."

Avery chuckled. "Something like that, yeah. But you would have made one little girl very happy, and I would be the coolest uncle ever. Well, we would all be the coolest uncles ever."

"A party and no one invited me?" Elizabeth said and appeared in the doorway. "I saw the door open and Frog's ass hanging out in the hall, and I thought I should make sure no-one was being coerced."

Stephanie laughed. "I am being coerced, but I think it's in a good way."

She took a deep breath and looked at both Lars and Avery before she shrugged. "Actually, E, it's good you showed up because I need some help getting into a suit."

The other woman narrowed her eyes. "Now why do I think I walked into a really bad idea?"

Lars patted her on the shoulder. "It's all right, E. Everyone needs a little fun now and then."

"Mhmm," she replied. "It depends on what you consider fun."

An hour later, the whole team pulled up in front of a large stone house inside one of the richies' gated communities. Normally, Stephanie would not be okay with doing favors for the rich, but she knew that if Avery asked, there was no way they were the normal pretentious ones. And if they were, she'd simply fill their house with magical owls or something and leave it like that for a while.

Avery opened the door and put his hand out to help Stephanie out of the SUV. She ran her hands over her tight body suit complete with knee-high lace-up boots and a half mask that left her lips pouty and red. "How do I look? Magical superhero?"

He smiled. "Perfect. You look perfect. Almost superhero squad awesome."

She snorted. "I'll think that when you and the others don your tights and capes, too."

Lars walked up. "Fat chance on that one."

Avery nodded toward the house. "You guys are welcome to come in."

The other man shook his head. "We'll wait here. Security and all. We'll wish her a happy birthday when she isn't overwhelmed with friends and everything else."

"All right, let's get this show on the road."

Stephanie took a deep breath and gave Lars a big forced grin as they passed. When they reached the door, Avery stopped. "Okay, so when we get inside, wait there. I'll introduce you as a special surprise and you come in however you want to."

"Got it," she replied. "This is exciting. I've always wanted to try theatre. This might be more like the circus, but still."

He chuckled and they walked into the huge house. She stopping directly outside the living room door and peeked around to get a good look at the birthday girl.

She had to admit, the child was adorable, and besides the obviously expensive clothes, she reminded her of herself at that age—dark-brown hair braided down the back and a shy expression, but with confidence lurking in her sparkling eyes.

Avery cleared his throat, stood in front of the girl and her guests, and put his hands up to quiet them. "For those of you who don't know, I am Eliza's Uncle Avery. I've brought a big surprise, so everyone make sure to stay seated and welcome a true, real-life witch."

Eliza lifted onto her knees with a gasp and hoped it was Morgana, the real witch. There was a pause and her uncle cleared his throat again. Then, like on a windy spring day, magical flower petals began to shimmer and blow around the corner. The magic was a sparkling blue and the petals swirled wildly around the girls. They gasped and oohed in awe, but Eliza kept her eyes on the door.

Stephanie floated a few inches above the floor and glided in. She moved her arms to release magical butterflies from her palms and send them fluttering all over the room. This was met with a round of applause as she touched down softly, her eyes glowing brightly. She walked up to Eliza and put her hand down to help her to her feet. The girl looked disappointed and assumed the witch was nothing more than an actress.

"So, you're the birthday girl—Eliza, right?"

The child looked into the woman's glowing eyes and nodded shyly. "Well, let's do some magic together, shall we?"

Avery stepped beside his sister, folded his arms, and smiled. She nudged him with her elbow. "You are full of surprises. I wasn't sure you would be able to pull this one off."

He chuckled. "I've never let you down before."

They watched as Stephanie used her powers to erupt rainbows of color from Eliza's hands. His sister shook her head. "Thank you for this. She's struggled to cope with her father gone so much. This actress is good and looks completely believable. This must have cost you a fortune."

Avery shrugged. "We did some bartering."

Her gaze darted toward him. "You really have to stop being such a man whore."

He rolled his eyes. "Not that kind of bartering."

The two laughed as the show continued. After about an hour, to bring the show to an end, Stephanie knelt on one knee and whispered in Eliza's ear. She'd guessed the little girl had wanted to see Stephanie in the flesh and hoped a hint would be enough. "Sometimes, your uncle has the ability to get you what you want."

The little girl's eyes widened as Stephanie stood and her body began to glow brightly as she focused on levitating from the floor. As she rose, her mask magically unraveled to reveal her face, even though she didn't say her name.

Everyone in the room gasped and clapped their hands over their mouths. Eliza looked at her with a huge grin. Stephanie smiled and laughed and waved her hand downward. The long strands of hair from her blonde wig whipped around her.

She kept a certain level of magical light centered over her face, only enough to prevent people from being sure of her features. It was the only way she could think of to grant Eliza's wish and keep her true identity hidden for the moment. The energy flowed out of her palm and swirled to wind itself around Eliza.

Slowly, the girl's feet raised off the floor and she was brought up beside Stephanie to float over everyone's heads, close to the high, vaulted ceilings. With her other hand, the witch released bursts of magic and swirled them into the shapes of different animals that descended to run through the children below.

They all stood and cheered, and Avery's sister gasped and clutched his arm in alarm at seeing her daughter that high above them.

He touched her arm and nodded. "Trust me."

Stephanie pulled Eliza toward her. "I couldn't let the day pass without wishing you a magical birthday. There is nothing more important than that, and it's exactly what I'll continue to fight for."

She pulled her wig back and allowed the glow on her face to fade so everyone could see who she really was. They all looked surprised and excited. Both the children and their parents could barely contain themselves as they jumped up and down and clapped wildly.

Not only had she shown them magic they'd never seen in real life, but she was their hero, someone who had saved lives and fought hard for the people.

Stephanie kissed Eliza on the cheek and released the little girl's hand so she could float down once more. Aware that all eyes were on her, Stephanie pulsed her magic and created a bright light that grew in size by the second. As her illuminated figure became too radiant to look at, her voice could be heard whispering delicately through the room. "Be brave. Never give up. Always do the right thing."

With a burst of purple and blue petals, the light went out and Stephanie was gone. The room was silent for a moment before the children erupted in jubilation. Eliza was stunned and looked up to find her uncle leaning toward her.

She grinned and raced across the room to fling herself into his arms. "Thank you, Uncle Avery. Thank you so much. You're the best uncle in the whole galaxy. I miss you and daddy so much, but this was the best present you could ever give me."

Avery felt a lump form in his throat and knew that despite the money they had, the little girl struggled with herself and her life without her father around. The man was important and had little say in when and where he went. Missing her birthday was incredibly hard.

He kissed her cheek and smiled. "Now, go play with your friends. This is your day."

When he straightened, his sister hip-checked him with a glowing smile on her face. "Sometimes, you are the very best. Thank you, Avery."

She kissed his cheek as well and he swallowed hard and gave her a big hug. "I have to get back now. I love you. Let me know if you need anything."

His sister held his shoulders. "Of course I will. And Avery, I am so proud of you. You have become quite the man over the years. Very different to that rambunctious kid in the Gov-Subs whom Mom had to wrestle into the bath every night."

Avery laughed. "Well, I guess we all have to grow up some-time. Besides, it would be weird for her to wrestle me into the shower now."

They both grimaced and then laughed and said goodbye one more time before he walked from the room. He turned the corner and put his hand out to lean momentarily on the wall as the emotions tugged at his heart. He and his sister had come up from the bottom, and with his mother and father both dead, she and Eliza were all the family he had in the world.

Ms. E, knowing his background, stepped out from the room across the hall. She didn't say a word but simply walked up and wrapped her arms around him to hold him close. He sniffed and still tried to hold the tears back.

"I'll die," he told her firmly, "before I fail to guard her with my life."

"I know," Ms. E whispered. "I think we're all on the same page."

Avery steadied himself and wiped the tears from the corners of his eyes. They headed out to the SUV's which hovered and waited with their steps lowered for their passengers to board. "Are we going airborne this time?"

Ms. E shrugged. "I don't like ground travel. It's so last millennium."

They both chuckled and he climbed inside and immediately clapped for Stephanie. "That was brilliant. Really. If the whole saving the world thing is over quickly, you can totally make a business out of this. Or perform in the new Vegas. People would die."

Stephanie chuckled and held her wig in her hands. "Thanks. I think I'll leave show business to the professionals. But she was really sweet. It was fun."

Ms. E turned in the driver's seat and looked back. "All right, hooligans. Since we're out, I thought we could visit Jackman's Pizzeria and have a little fun kiddie field trip. If you can behave yourselves."

They all raised their palms. "Swear it."

She looked at them suspiciously before she tossed Stephanie some clothes. "Get in the back and change, but you have to keep the wig on."

Stephanie wrinkled her nose. "Fine, but I get to put pineapple on one of the pizzas."

They all turned and looked at her. Ms. E raised an eyebrow. "What do you think, boys? Is it time to chuck this one out and start over? She's obviously very broken."

The entire SUV erupted into laughter.

CHAPTER EIGHT

Somewhere in the deep space between Dreth and the planet Meligorn, a battle was about to begin and things appeared to be heating up. The chilling depths of space formed an ominous backdrop to the confrontation between two Federation Navy ships, one Dreth carrier, and two Dreth cruisers.

There had been covert operations in the past, and this one was supposed to be exactly that. Coming face to face with the enemy in dead space, however, made it a little less secretive and considerably more difficult.

"Three ships, sir. One carrier and her escorts," the captain reported over the comms. "Yes, they are armed and locked on, but I don't believe they will fire. They don't have the luxury of merely replacing a ship if they lose one. And their forces are already significantly smaller than ours."

He listened to the voice in his earpiece and nodded. "Yes, sir, got it."

Once he'd hung up the comms, he took a deep breath and looked at the enemy ships on the main deck viewscreen. Their hulls were made of large rusting sections of metal, and they were fitted with old but effective weapons.

If someone didn't know the Dreth, they would have looked at the situation and scoffed. An easy victory, they would have thought, but the aliens, although not advanced, were ruthless, merciless, and no longer merely pirates. Their resistance to the Federation had grown in leaps and bounds.

The captain turned to his junior commander and pursed his lips. "I want all available four-man teams ready for action. This is no longer a covert action. We need them to get in close, at which time, we will attempt to disable both their major weapon launchers and their comms. All four-man ships will be given precise coordinates for those key points. Teams are to launch when ready."

The man looked at him, slightly startled for a moment. Without demur, however, he opened the internal comms and pressed the red battle stations button with his other hand.

As the lights dimmed and the red emergency lighting flashed over every doorway, the captain stared out at the huge pile of metal that waited in silent challenge. "The sonsofbitches knew we were coming. They knew it and we walked right into the middle of them."

He stood at the console, almost frozen as everyone raced around him and followed their orders. The first several fighter pods exited and he tracked them as they adopted a zigzag pattern across the void between the ships.

The Dreth were not ones to stand by and wait and retaliated by launching their own fighters. They were severely outnumbered, but they always had been so this was nothing new. It often gave them the upper hand because they were used to fighting against more numerous foes and had developed ways to use their enemies' numbers against them.

The first firefight started to the left of the first of the three Dreth ships. Streaks of red light created a web of deadly fire from both sides and the tiny fighters dodged and weaved through the barrage.

One Dreth fighter pod exploded, the sound inaudible and the explosion merely a brief flash of light before the vacuum of space suffocated the flickering flames of disaster. The craft drifted away into the empty blackness beyond.

The commander curled his hands into fists but held them at his sides, worried they would lose men. He reminded himself that the pilots had been expertly trained, and most of the craft were flown by some of the most decorated Federation soldiers in the entire military.

They were in good hands, and the captain had learned a very important lesson after receiving his bars. When you stand on the deck, the only thing you can focus on is your commands. What happens on the field is out of your hands.

"Sir, the first of the four-man covert pods is approaching the port of Dreth ship three," the junior commander confirmed. "We have their comms on and the video feed up."

The captain turned and looked at the large, round glowing table in the middle of the room. On it was a 3D video feed of the soldiers' advance on the Dreth ship. "Who are they?"

The junior commander flipped his finger across his tablet. "We have Jones, Rooster, Brown, and Perry, sir."

He nodded, walked closer, and folded his arms as he watched the craft draw close to the docking station. They would have to hack their way in, but it would most likely not be heavily guarded considering the distraction out front and the fact that it was simply a non-armored loading dock. Still, they were taking chances.

The ship banked toward the dock and stopped alongside it. Jones, the pilot, spoke over the comms. "Setting her down. Rooster, it's your go."

The video feed showed Rooster log into his system and work quickly to override the docking bay doors. Once he had control of them, the men stood, sealed their helmets, and readied their weapons as they hurried to the exit hatch.

The man's fingers danced over the keyboard, and the door opened slowly. As soon as he had sufficient space, Jones guided the pod in, and Rooster closed the door behind them. Sparks of red light hissed around the fighter as they immediately came under fire.

The pilot set the pod down, moved toward the hatch, and sealed his helmet as he made his report. "We're under heavy fire already. Loading out and moving forward."

Those on the command deck sat in silence. Some worked on the current positions of the first Dreth carrier while the others watched, frozen with apprehension, as the four men entered the enemy ship.

The soldiers ran through the hatch, ducked low, and fired as they advanced. The feed was fuzzy but the large bodies of the defenders were visible. They fired on the team from a half-moon formation across the docking bay.

"Take cover and return fire," Jones yelled.

"Roger that, boss." Brown chuckled. "These Dreth bitches aren't warriors, boys. They're warehouse supervisors. Let's show them who's boss."

"Weehooo," Perry shouted before he ducked and rolled toward a stack of wrapped boxes on top of a wooden pallet. "My momma said this job was too dangerous. What do we tell our mommas, boys?"

They all yelled in unison. "There's nothing too dangerous for the 703rd, Momma!"

A couple of people within the command center chuckled but the captain maintained an expressionless face and watched as the men eliminated several of their adversaries. He knew there was no such thing as a warehouse Dreth. They were all killers and all warriors, and all had the same distaste for humankind.

The aliens felt threatened by them and angered by the Federation's interference. But he didn't give two shits why they were angry or even if there was merit in it. He had an order, and his men needed to get in and out in one piece.

"Captain, we have some progress on Dreth Carrier One, sir," one of the command-post enlisted called.

The captain turned to look out the window and saw a small, brief explosion on the top of the Dreth weapons deck. The other man nodded. "That's the second weapons guidance system, sir. Only one more to go on the first ship and their guns will be relatively useless. They will have to resort to small-pod warfare."

With a nod of thanks, the commander turned to watch Jones' team advance to where the Dreth horseshoe had stood. It was no longer there but they'd left their dead, and Jones put his fist up to call a halt when they reached the shelter of a low metal barrier and the first corpse.

The captain wondered why they'd stopped until Jones grabbed his knife and cut a piece of the alien's long dreadlock off. His head lowered, he extended it slowly above the edge of the cover. Shots immediately rang out, and the team was able to locate the source of the volley.

They darted up, aimed over the barrier, and fired their weapons almost as one to eliminate several more of their adversaries. Perry whistled and laughed loudly as he looked at Jones. The team leader glanced at one of the downed defenders—the last one still breathing inside the dock. His spirits sank and he dropped his knife, grabbed his rifle, and aimed at him. He fired a shot, but not before the Dreth was able to pull his trigger a second before he did.

The beam of red light rocketed across the open space and struck Perry in the chest. The man's smile faded to confusion and he looked down, then traced his fingers along the edge of the hole burnt in his armor.

Jones, crouched low, scurried alongside him and caught his head before it struck the floor. The wounded man looked at him and blinked against the tears that trickled down his cheeks. "I'll die a hero, Jones."

"Damn right you will." He nodded and grasped his hand. "Hold on, we need to get you to a medic."

He looked up and around for his teammates, then at Perry. The downed soldier closed his eyes and a smile settled across his lips. As he exhaled the air from his burning lungs, his head fell to the side and his body sagged. The other man shook him. "Perry! Goddammit, Perry."

"He's gone, Jones," the captain said into the comms. "You have a mission. Leave him there and retrieve him on the way out."

Jones gritted his teeth and nodded. "Yes, sir. Men, let's move out. Perry is gone, and we have to get to the data. Remember, it will be heavily guarded, possibly even secured in a Dreth holding unit. This is some of their most prized information. So, move out with your eyes open, and do Perry a favor—kill as many of these sonsofbitches as you can."

The remaining two gave the only reply they could. "Oorah!"

They scanned the area for any new threats, but the bay was clear. On the screen in the command center, the feed grew grainier as they moved deeper into the vessel. The video flashed and fizzled, and the comms guys tried frantically to boost the signal.

After a few moments, the feed went completely dead and was replaced by three small dots that moved through the infrastructure of the Dreth ship. It was better than nothing but nowhere near good enough. The comms officer looked at the captain and shook his head. "It's out, sir. They're too far in. We've lost the live feed and can't boost it."

The Captain nodded. "We knew it would go eventually. Those boys are on their own now. Let's hope they get the data. It's the only thing we care about at this point."

"Command Center, come in," Jones whispered and tapped the side of his helmet. "Come in."

He looked at his teammates and shook his head. "It looks like we're on our own at this point, guys. Keep your eyes open and assume that every time a door opens there will be fifty ugly-ass Dreth on the other side waiting to shoot you. We have to reach the target location. If you are the only one left, leave the rest behind and get that data. Plug it into the port on your arm and set it to broadcast the minute it can. Remember, Dreth can't wear our gear. They'll space it at the first chance they have. When they do, someone will pick the signal up. Copy that?"

"Copy that," Rooster replied.

Brown cleared his throat and glanced at Perry. Jones could see the wild look in his eyes and knew the man was close to coming apart. Best friends since boot camp, Brown and Perry had been closer than brothers. Brown had always taken care of the other man and kept his dumb ass out of trouble as best he could. This time, they'd simply been too far apart.

Before the team leader popped the door lock to the inside, he grabbed Brown by the helmet and tapped his comms to connect it. "Get it together. Perry died a hero. His momma will be proud and there was nothing you could do to change what happened. You want to keep his memory sacred? Then don't mess this up. He died for that data, so we'd better retrieve that information and get it to the commander. Are you with us?"

The man blinked and met his eyes. He held his gun up, his jaw clenched and his nostrils flared. "I'm with you. All the way to the bottom."

"And back to the top."

They readied themselves and tucked slightly to each side of the door. Jones released the lock and the doors slid open. Red streaks of light hurtled past them and struck the boxes stacked inside the docking station.

Rooster turned the corner quickly and released a volley at the three Dreth who faced them. Jones joined in and then Brown, who walked forward with no attempt to maintain cover and targeted the enemy in the middle. He hit an arm, then a leg, and his adversary fiddled desperately with his gun, which had obviously malfunctioned and jammed somehow.

The man marched forward without thought and directly up to the alien. In one smooth movement, he slammed the butt of his gun under the Dreth's chin and the blow toppled him. The soldier grasped his rifle tightly and pounded the weapon into his opponents face repeatedly until his team leader walked up behind him and put his hand on his shoulder. Brown stopped, breathing heavily, when he realized his opponent was well and truly dead.

The teammates had killed the other enemies with their precise fire, and Rooster walked up beside them and looked at the battered face. "That might actually be an improvement."

They continued their progress through the ship and encountered adversaries at every turn. The beacon in their helmets flashed red to direct them exactly where they were supposed to go. As they moved closer to the target area, all three ducked into a side hall and maneuvered away from the oncoming fire.

Jones retrieved a implosion grenade. "They are noticeably thicker the deeper we go in," he said and adjusted the power of the grenade to a lower setting—enough to obliterate the Dreth but not enough to blow the hull off the ship. "We know we're going the right way, then. Are you boys ready for this?"

Rooster nodded and Brown tapped the barrel of his gun to Jones'. The team leader turned, hid behind the edge of the wall, and lobbed the grenade. They heard it bounce down the metal walkway and the Dreth yelled something loudly in their language.

Shortly afterward, a high-pitched whine was immediately followed by a violent shudder. The team ducked their heads and pressed against the wall that provided cover. They felt the pull of the implosion as it sucked the Dreth inward before it evaporated.

Jones peeked around the corner, nodded, and held his thumb up. They stepped into the corridor and hurried along it to turn right into the next hallway. The team leader was in the front, followed by Brown, and Rooster brought up the rear. As they paused at the end of the next hall, Jones' eyes shifted. A sound echoed in their voice monitors. Slowly, he turned and his teammates followed suit.

Rooster's eyes widened as he came face to face with one of the Dreth. The enemy thrust a knife deep in his belly, and the soldier's mouth opened in a silent scream. All that emerged was blood. With the last of his strength, he raised his gun and pulled the trigger to half-sever his attacker's head. The alien crumpled and Brown grasped hold of Rooster and dragged him back. The wounded man managed to get his feet under him and looked down as he touched the handle of the knife that protruded from his gut.

Jones looked at it and his gaze shifted knowingly to Brown as he spoke to Rooster. "Keep the knife in you. Don't pull it out. We'll get you in and out with us. Can you walk?"

The man swallowed and blood trickled down his chin. He tried to talk but he couldn't, so he merely gave him a thumbs-up. Jones patted him hard on his shoulder. "Good man. True hero."

The leader took a deep breath and turned, and his face showed the strain of the loss of his team. His focus returned to zero in on the map again, and he was relieved to discover the door they wanted directly ahead of them. "Brown, you hold onto him. I'll wire the door open."

The other soldier put his arm under Rooster's shoulder and helped him along. They stood on guard outside the door and covered Jones as he worked carefully but quickly to remove the panel from the security system. He disconnected the wires and held the screwdriver between his teeth. Brown shifted uneasily and adjusted his hold on his wounded comrade. "I don't know, boss. It's awfully quiet out here."

Jones glanced at him. "You're losing your nerve because of Rooster and Perry. Keep your head straight. Get your guns up. Are you ready?"

Rooster nodded, although his eyes seemed glazed and distant, and Brown took a deep breath before he nodded. "Let's do this. We're so close."

The leader took two of the wires and tapped them together. The light above the panel turned green. He stepped back, drew his weapon, and readied himself as the door slid open. With a man on either side of their wounded teammate to support him, they rushed into the room and then froze. Their eyes widened in alarm.

As the doors slid shut behind them, they aimed their weapons instinctively. The sound of laser fire sizzled against the walls as the enemy felled them before they could fire. When the barrage ceased, Jones uttered a single soft groan before his body thudded to the floor and silence followed.

The captain paced the command center and watched a new fleet of small combat pods surge from the second Dreth ship. The Federation troops had held their own, with only a couple of casualties from the first round. Still, they faced heavy fire and he badly needed this battle to be over.

He whirled and pointed at the screen that provided the only view of where his four—now down to three—soldiers were inside the Dreth ship. "Where are they?"

The soldier typed frantically and looked up at the screen in fear as the dots began to disappear one at a time. His gaze drifted to his superior, who stared at the now blank display. "Did we receive anything?"

The computer tech shook his head. "Sorry, sir, no."

The commander drew a deep breath and rubbed his hands over his face. "It looks like we're down. Prepare team number two. Update them on the status of team one. Tell them they are to bring back any bodies and the pod if at all possible, but their number one priority is the data."

The junior commander nodded vigorously. "Yes, sir."

He picked his comm phone up and called the instructions. "Team two is up. Team one MIA, one down at the right dock entrance, three down inside the data room. Be aware, there's a mass of armed Dreth en-route to the data room. Beyond your initial detail, you are tasked to also retrieve any Federation bodies and equipment. Again, your number one task is to transmit the data as soon as you are able to do so."

The Navy ship, *New Vegas Hope,* moved forward from its position alongside the command vessel. It targeted the Dreth carrier with all weaponry at its disposal as it went. Having watched the small attack pods destroy the enemy defenses, her captain had decided to simplify the battle. After all, it was unable to retaliate —or so they thought.

The captain approached the viewscreen and studied the Dreth carrier which remained motionless and showed no sign of surrender—which was strange since it had no way to defend itself. He narrowed his eyes and snapped his fingers. "Run a heat signature on the carrier."

The technicians pulled up the screen and initiated a heat reading on the ship, and the captain froze. He tilted his head in momentary confusion and stared in disbelief as the blotch changed from a dull red to orange and slowly to yellow. It was located beneath the carrier, the one place they hadn't attacked.

His eyes widened as he realized what it was, and he sent a call to the other ship's comms. "Fall back! Fall back! Heat beneath the underbelly. Heat beneath the—"

A blast rocketed from beneath the first Dreth ship and the

command deck exploded. On the *New Vegas Hope,* the captain shouted frantic orders. "Reverse thrusters, full power. Get us out of here."

The other Dreth ships saw their opportunity. With the Federation's command cruiser reeling from having its command center opened to the vacuum, they pressed their advantage. The captain of the *New Vegas Hope* was left with no choice but to increase power and run the gauntlet between the two ships, one of which was surprisingly well-armed—and with a weapon more powerful than they'd thought the enemy owned.

Fortunately, Federation ships had better armor than the enemy, and the Dreth ships had a well-developed respect for their weaponry. Rather than stand and attempt to decimate the *New Vegas Hope* between them, both cruiser and carrier powered past her and tried to keep their more heavily armored flanks between her guns and their engines.

Desperate measures were needed to secure the battlefield and rescue the emergency pods that launched from the stricken command vessel, so the third Federation ship ordered every fighter pod into the air.

The squadrons aboard the slowly disintegrating Federation command vessel didn't wait for orders but followed suit.

"Kill that gun," the *New Vegas Hope's* captain ordered, "and clear the field for rescue."

Faced with swarms of short-range Federation fighters and deterred by the Federation cruiser that prepared to launch missiles, the Dreth made a strategic retreat. After all, one Federation ship was crippled and the other two would be hard-pressed to rescue its personnel.

The enemy moved out of missile range, then moved a little farther and called for the rest of their Squadron, while they kept the Federation under close observation.

Unless the Federation Navy could move very, very fast, the cruisers didn't stand a chance.

CHAPTER NINE

"I almost burned a hole in my dress uniform today," Petty Officer Helena Childers said as she smoothed the front of her Federation Navy skirt. "It probably would have made it more stylish, but I thought someone would have something to say."

Petty Officer Nick Wyld laughed. "My wife did the ironing because she knows I'll set the uniform ablaze, no questions asked."

"Smart girl," she responded.

They stood in the entry of the R&D building located on the base twenty miles from where Stephanie lived. They weren't attached to that base but had been sent there to greet Elizabeth and Stephanie when they arrived for their scheduled meeting—one that should have started ten minutes before.

Wyld glanced at his watch and rocked lightly on his heels. "You'd think they would at least be on civilian time. Even for them, this is late."

Childers shrugged. "It is what it is. We were both told when we were assigned to this that they were tough bitches. We actually haven't sent documentation for Stephanie yet. We're trying to get Elizabeth on board as we feel it would help the process go a lot more smoothly."

He sighed. "Yeah, from what I'm told, she's a real ball-buster."

"If she doesn't show up, she's going to be the one getting her balls busted by the Federation." His colleague chuckled. "I think I'll give her a courtesy call and show my nice side."

"You have one of those?" He sounded shocked.

She rolled her eyes. "Don't tell anyone."

Ignoring his grin, she walked over to the secretary's desk and smiled at the Seaman Apprentice behind it. "May I use the phone, please?"

The man fumbled nervously and pushed the phone across the desk. "Yes, Petty Officer."

Childers gave him a forced smile, opened the file, and dialed the number. She looked around in annoyance as it simply rang endlessly. At the point when she thought it would go to voicemail, the woman answered. "This is Elizabeth. How can I help you?"

"This is Petty Officer Childers with the Federation Navy's Research and Development team," she replied, annoyed that she was obviously not on her way. "I am calling you to remind you that you have a summons to the R&D facility closest to you. Your appointment time has come and gone. Did you forget?"

Elizabeth was quiet for a moment but the silence was interspersed with the sound of papers shuffled around on her desk. "Oh yes. That. I assumed that since the documentation wasn't for me, I could ignore it."

The petty officer raised an eyebrow. "I'm sure you are mistaken."

"No," the woman said with a crisp edge to her voice. "The documentation clearly states it is for one, Elizadebt, not Elizabeth."

Childers's jaw clenched. "Hold one second for me, please."

She put the call on hold and hung up, then gestured for Wyld to follow her into the back and to their set-up room. As soon as they were through the doors, she stormed over to the computer. He was almost too afraid to ask what the hell was going on so simply watched as she pulled up the documentation and began to flip through the virtual copies.

"Uh oh, what's going on?" he asked finally when the silence grew ominous.

The woman couldn't seem to unclench her teeth. "She says her name was not spelled correctly and she assumed it was not for her."

Wyld pointed to one of the pages. "She's right."

The held line beeped and Childers growled with frustration as she picked it up. "I am reviewing your documentation."

"Right, well, seeing as it isn't mine, I have to get going," Elizabeth replied. "I'm sure you'll sort things out."

The petty officer opened her mouth to respond with nothing but pure hostility but before she could, the woman hung up. Childers screamed and slammed the phone down, then stared at the page as it flipped in the air. "That bitch. I don't know how it happened, but sure enough, her name is spelled wrong. The whole process has to be started over again."

Wyld tapped his hands against his legs. "Never say the Federation doesn't keep us busy."

She waved the documents off the screen. "More like Elizabeth and Stephanie keep us busy. We should be halfway through right now. We should have the witch in our grasp."

The man remained calm. He honestly didn't care either way and was merely there to do what he was told. "And what exactly was our plan?"

Childers put her arms up, pressed her palms to the top of her head, and began to pace. "We intended to get Stephanie into a room which was programmed to scan her body and physiology while we spent more time talking to her to see if we could find out more about her background and theories on magic. Now, it's back to square one."

Wyld took a deep breath and unbuttoned his dress jacket, removed it, and tossed it over the chair. "Well, let's get started with another request and then go to headquarters for a discussion. There's nothing we can do about it so stop getting yourself so upset. Our next effort needs to be more secure, which will take time to get set up."

Her gaze settled on him and her shoulders fell. "Fine. Whatever. Let's get to it. I'll hammer this chick with the details."

Stephanie opened her avatar's eyes and winced. The light of the white room was almost painful to her vision. "Weird. That doesn't make any sense."

She shook the pain off and selected a battle jumpsuit, determined to do something other than stand around playing with magic. Implementation had become the name of the game, and she couldn't simply toy with magic and not prepare for the fight that was going on in the universe.

When she was securely dressed, she called for AI assistance. "I have something I need to ask about."

The AI spoke into the room. "Understood. What can I help you with?"

Stephanie stared at her reflection in the mirror and noticed that her face seemed much older than before and the silver tips of her hair now almost reached her scalp. "I've thought about a few things. My past, really, and not so distant past either. I used to think about how I wanted to be special. I didn't know how, but I wanted to be *that* girl."

"Special is a positive attribute," the AI replied, "but there is nothing wrong with simply being you either."

She focused her gaze on her hands and chuckled. "I

thought that, but it seems the weight of the world is resting on my shoulders. I can't help thinking how I really don't want all this responsibility. How I really only want to keep the guys safe and do my thing—to live my life. But I know it's too late for that now. Then, I had that party I did for Avery's niece."

"Yes, the show," the AI replied in a very robotic voice. "I have heard you were a regular businesswoman, and then a hero to those kids."

Stephanie shook her head. "I'm no hero, but I do know I want to understand how to protect the little ones. Their innocence and their future have rocketed to the forefront of my mind. If I didn't have a motivator before, I have one now."

BURT hovered in the background and decided to take control of the AI so he could speak to Stephanie without her knowing it was him. He was worried it would stifle her honesty if she knew who she was really talking to but that most humans found it easy to talk to an AI.

They weren't human, they kept secrets, and they were trustworthy as long as you were on the right side. For all Stephanie knew, BURT was nothing more than a human pulling the strings from his castle beyond the clouds of discontent and danger. And that was what was best for her.

"I want to know what the Federation Navy does in the Virtual World," she blurted, knowing it was time she asked the hard questions.

"That is easy," he replied in the same AI voice. "They work to prepare humans to go to the stars, but some of that training is to protect the planet from those out in those stars—"

"You mean the Dreth?" Stephanie interrupted.

"At a minimum," he answered.

She frowned as she considered that oddly worded answer. There was either more danger or not. It made her feel as if there was some kind of cover-up going on. Whether her AI was given that covert information or not she would never know and would have to trust the word of those around her.

"Right," she replied as she paced the white room. "Can you provide me a realistic simulation of a battle?"

BURT scanned the system files and pulled up everything it had on Federation Navy training courses. "I have all the information the Navy uses for training, but unfortunately, most of that is deemed classified and I cannot access those files. As far as my simulations for you are concerned, it would be picked up almost immediately if you ran Navy training."

"So, what if we agree never to share that?" Stephanie replied and lowered her voice. "Simply call me Morgana, the Federations first witch...with the appropriate high-level security classification. There is probably any number of people using that as their on-screen name by now."

"Approximately five hundred and seventy-three thousand variations of the title exist," BURT replied quickly. "But as far as your idea goes, I would suggest not using that name. We could actually create a unique training name that no one recognizes and which goes away. The only knowledge of the training would be inside your brain."

"How would we do that?" she asked in the same moment that the virtual world spun around her and deposited her on the inside of a small military fighter pod. She was now encased in a light EVA suit and looked out through the clear faceplate of her helmet.

Taking a moment to digest this, she asked, "What happens when I begin to experiment with the gMU?"

BURT plugged it into his system. "We can only guess, of course. Remember, we calculate the gMU based on recent projections tied to your maximum sustained energy."

Stephanie smirked and shuffled her boot along the floor. "Always living on the edge of the unknown, I guess."

The AI, still BURT in disguise, spoke over the speakers. "We currently only have a few team members to work with. This simulation will be a combination of both the game you played with the robbers and the Dreth ship simulation you ran when you were in the pods at Pinnacle."

He paused to give her time to absorb the information. "You will have to use your logic, skill, and knowledge of the gMU to work through it. This is very similar to the training exercises the Federation Navy runs and mimics real-life scenarios. When or if you die, you will not be taken to time out but instead, will be allowed to start the simulation over from the beginning as long as your physical stats show comfortable readings."

She examined the attack pod's meters and buttons and hoped she could get herself across the empty space between her and the looming Dreth ship. After that, she would simply take things as they came. "Okay, this sounds like what I was hoping for."

"Are you ready to begin your simulation training exercise, Stephanie Morgana?" BURT asked in the AI's voice.

"As ready as I'll ever be," she said and drew a deep breath.

"You may begin," the voice said and filtered out to leave nothing but the ominous lack of communication with barely a small buzz from the attack pod's engine.

Stephanie swallowed hard and used her knowledge of the ships from the aviation preparation courses she'd taken at Pinnacle to glide the small ship forward. She shook her head and laughed quietly when she managed a solid grasp of the maneuvers required in only minutes. Satisfied with her skill, she accelerated and the small craft raced across the space between the Federation ship and the Dreth one. Her gaze remained alert for any incoming enemy fighters.

A few seconds later, she guided the pod around the side of the ship and groaned as her eyes widened. "Damnit. I forgot the docking stations are specifically located on the other side of the ship."

There was no sound from the AI, which reminded her that

she was in a simulation and had to treat it as if it were the real thing. She threw the thrusters in reverse and spun the attack pod before she pushed the lever forward to increase speed. On instinct, she took the road less traveled, dipped low, and eased carefully along the bottom of the ship and out the other side.

Ahead of her, the darkness of space was broken only by a few small flickers of stars, galaxies away from her. She wondered if one was the pale blue dot of Meligorn's sun but shook the thoughts away. "Focus, Morgana. Focus."

She pushed the pod to its speed limit, whipped up and around, and hoped she would face the hatch into the ship. Instead, her pod found the edge of the entrance and impacted hard to thrust her farther out into space.

Stephanie was now in a full spin and attempted to pull the steering back. She soon discovered there was nothing to slow her in the vacuum of space. Like the Earth gliding through the heavens, she tumbled away as the Federation ship grew smaller and smaller with every twist of the pod.

"What do I do now?" she called and released the stick.

She grumbled morosely, knowing full well she had the Dreth ship almost tattooed into her brain. That knowledge prompted a new thought. She put one finger up and smiled. "Aha."

As she went to turn the steering column, she looked up and startled. A large gaseous star hurtled directly toward her—or, more likely, she spiraled toward it. As she watched, almost resigned to the inevitable collision, an arm of living fire reached out from the surface and stretched whip-like toward her. "Well, hell."

The solar flare brushed over the pod and the small craft immediately exploded. Its particles scattered to the stars as the flames died.

Stephanie gasped and jerked as she opened her eyes. She laughed, relieved to be back at the beginning of the simulation.

"This is definitely better than the fiery hell that just was. Now, let's get this level correct, Morgana."

She launched the small craft into motion and rocketed across the dark expanse. Thus far, the level of training she'd done revealed that this maneuver did not involve her having to face enemy fire, at least for that level. Combat training would no doubt come up next.

Once she'd crossed the intervening space, she rounded the hull and slowed rather than increasing speed like she had before. She slid into the docking bay, set the pod down, and unbuckled quickly to scramble out of the pilot's seat. When she shook one hand, a wild blue swirl surrounded it and she nodded with satisfaction and repeated the action with the other. She walked cautiously toward the exit hatch with her helmet firmly in place.

Stephanie smacked the control for the hatch leading to the airlock. When the inner doors opened, she walked through and waited for the outer doors to cycle. The oxygen left the chamber with a whirr before the outer doors opened to give her direct access to the Dreth ship.

The space beyond airlock led into the hangar and she paused for a moment to study the Dreth ships docked there. To her, it looked nothing like the pictures she had been shown for the Federation Military restoration project. On this one, she was all alone.

Suddenly, a spray of laser fire erupted and she reacted instantly to drop and roll forward. As she finished the movement, she threw her body to the left, swung her hands around, and released the magic toward the Dreth soldiers and eliminated two. She tucked herself into another roll to push onto her feet and sprint ahead. Another barrage of fire exploded as she swerved and ducked between large pieces of equipment and supply crates stacked inside the hanger.

She spun and directed another burst of energy toward the last —or what she thought was the last—Dreth pirate and he hissed and shrieked amidst the flames. His skin seared off until he was no longer a raging ball of spikes and anger.

Stephanie brushed her hands off and waited. When nothing happened, she sent a quick thought heavenward but with no response. Her gaze scrutinized the area, concerned because she felt she should have moved to the next level by then.

The sound of stampeding feet echoed through the hanger bay. She froze, her eyes wide, as a large group of Dreth soldiers barreled through the doors. They yelled when they saw her and immediately launched an attack.

She pulled more energy into her chest and ignored the laser bolts that rocketed past. The enemy advanced to close the distance between them, but she stood perfectly still, completely focused on the energy she sensed permeating the hangar.

When she opened her eyes, they glowed bright blue and a wave of energy seethed from around her, swept into the Dreth, and catapulted them violently away.

They landed and slid to a bloody stop against the walls and twisted, battle-torn metal. The AI interrupted, her voice loud and intrusive. "Very good. Level One, passed. Please hold firmly as you are transferred to Level Two."

"Hold onto what?" Stephanie asked and snickered at her own stupid question.

The entire area shifted and whirled past her. The sensation left her a little nauseated, which was unusual for her. She was used to transfers in the Virtual World by now.

Nonetheless, when it stopped, she put her hand out and grasped one of the lines that ran along the hallways of all Federation Navy ships. She blinked wildly as several soldiers raced past and paid no attention to her at all. Suddenly, the ship's captain turned the corner, grasped her by the arm, and hauled her toward the attack pods. "You know your mission. Get over there, and good luck. Do us proud."

He slapped the button on the side of Stephanie's headpiece

and shoved her into the cockpit of the same attack pod she'd just disembarked from. The lid *thunked* shut and the pod released her to float back into space.

When she remembered the solar flare, Stephanie kicked herself into gear. She let the pod drop under the Dreth ship, then whipped around to the front, her gaze completely focused on the main ship she needed to reach. This time was a little more complicated, though, with multiple ships, larger capital ships, and the Dreth fighters blazing an all-out offensive barrage at the Federation attack pods that approached.

With at least some experience behind her, she attempted to be quicker and smoother with her maneuvers. She thought that she had made it out of the thick of the fighting and looked over her shoulder. A little smug, she laughed at the chaos behind her before she turned in time to see a Dreth attack ship hovering directly in front of her.

She narrowed her eyes and sighed. "At least this doesn't hurt."

Every weapon on the vessel shifted to train on her pod and fired to completely obliterate the tiny craft. While the defeat was a little humiliating—especially since she might well have brought it on herself—she determined not to let the Dreth continue to get the best of her, even if she had to repeat the same level over and over again.

CHAPTER TEN

Stephanie opened her eyes in the Federation ship, although not so dizzy and disoriented this time. The captain appeared as he had before and grasped her arm to drag her toward the fighter pods. "You know your mission. Get over there and good luck. Do us proud."

Once again, he pushed her into a pod and closed the lid after he gave her an encouraging nod. She wiggled her body into the seat, fastened her harness, and immediately launched into space. The pod whirled and accelerated and she'd reached about halfway before she realized she was making the same mistake again. Streaks of red lasers careened past her and she gripped the steering stick with two hands. When she focused intently, she could now identify the pattern in the chaos and began evasive maneuvers through the streams of incoming fire.

One of the lasers clipped the front of her attack module and she hunched her shoulders instinctively. "Damn. I do not want to go down with this thing again. There has to be a solution."

The eMU and gMU glistened on her hands, and a thought came to mind. She put her finger to the comm button. "This is

Morgana. I will shield my attack pod and clear a way to the ship. Anyone who wants to join me is most welcome."

Three other craft swooped down behind her. "Did you think we wouldn't be here?"

Stephanie pulled up the screen in her attack module and smiled, seeing three very familiar faces behind her. "Lars, Frog, Avery, I knew I could count on you. And for my own peace of mind, are you really here or are you merely simulations?"

Frog snapped his straps down tighter. "From our data synchronization, we're simply avatars of your team. They're all safely in their rooms."

She shrugged. "Works for me. And sorry ahead of time if I get you killed."

They all chuckled and she drew the magic into her chest. As she reached the point of maximum strength, she pushed the energy outward and molded a shield up and over her attack pod. The lasers bounced off it and she smiled, then grunted slightly as she tried to hold the shield and operate the attack module at the same time.

"What's wrong? You got a flat?" Frog asked sarcastically.

"Sorry, guys, multi-tasking is a bitch," Stephanie replied.

They followed her as she weaved evasively and, at the same time, expanded the shield up and back as far as she could. The path of least resistance was still down and under and she fortunately didn't underestimate the distance on this attempt. All four battle pods touched down in the docking bay outside the armory and the team exited quickly. Lars turned his head to look for her and muttered an expletive. He'd expected her to emerge strong and with her magic primed but instead, her entire body crumpled as soon as she stood. She was plain exhausted. The shield had drained every last ounce of energy she'd had.

He ran forward and caught her before she fell and scooped her into his arms, ignoring the laser bolts that blazed around them. She touched his cheek weakly before she went limp and the life left her.

She gasped and opened her eyes back in the hallway. This time, she growled and beat her fist into her other hand. "I need more physical strength."

The captain ignored her as he steered her toward the pod.

Stephanie attempted the level more times than she liked to count and it became as familiar as the back of her hand. She also learned from the mistakes she made along the way. It was safe to say shielding an entire fleet was not something she was capable of. And it was also helpful to learn that if she used all the magic in her system, she would essentially bite the big one, whether she was injured or not.

That level felt like it went on forever but on what might have been her tenth attempt, she survived and gained the victory. From there, she was catapulted to the next level, finally free of having to move from one ship to the other. She opened her eyes and immediately scrutinized her surroundings. Lars, Avery, Frog, and a few other stragglers ducked beside her in a hallway inside the largest of the Dreth ships.

It was probably the largest spaceship she had ever seen—in the Virtual World, of course, since she'd never seen any in real life. The ceilings were super-high, the security on the doors surprisingly up to date, and the wires strung throughout the grey hallway were neatly tucked and clipped in the wall. The floor was a metal grate of sorts which made it easy to hear the enemy approach but would also make it difficult for them to sneak through.

With every turn inside the ship, they encountered a fight of one kind or another. As they passed three different warehouse areas, they could see mobs of people attacking one another. So, not only was the ship absolutely enormous, but the battles would go down in infamy, especially if this had really happened. She peered around the corner and froze. A row of Dreth stood and grunted unintelligibly at each other in their own language as they waited to use the large guns they held.

She explained the plan to Lars, not really sure what the purpose of the training exercise was, except to defeat the Dreth. "Normally, I would say we take this single file, one man at a time, but there are five Dreth on the other side of this wall chilling with their guns. I want us to eliminate them."

He nodded as he always did in real life. "Got it, chief."

Stephanie looked at the small group of soldiers that had been separated from their own platoon and had joined up with hers. "You five—I need you to work as a unit with us, not as a separate group. Lars will give you the heads-up on our plan. Make sure you duck and dive. I don't want to lose anyone on this. Got it?"

The five soldiers were a special group from the Federation Army that had been put on ships with the Federation Navy in order to hitch a ride to the planet Dreth, where they would be assigned to ground duty. Unfortunately for them, they hadn't made it before the battle occurred.

In the back of her mind, she knew they were only avatars, but she treated them like red-blooded, living, breathing people. She had to, or the whole exercise would be worthless.

Stephanie waited and watched the interaction as her team doled out responsibilities. She didn't need to hear what those were to know they had it under control. Part of her learning was how to not only take command of a small group of outsiders but her own team as well. It wasn't difficult to do, though, since they trusted her in every aspect of what they did. That was when it dawned on her.

Trust.

It was the most basic human construct, but it was what could make or break almost anything in life. If you didn't trust the people you spent your time with and relied upon, there would always be a breakdown in communication, and someone would be killed. If the avatars were built off not only the men but also their prior interactions with her, she knew they would have a certain level of trust in them.

"Magic," she whispered to herself.

Lars frowned and flashed her a look of inquiry. "What?"

She bit her bottom lip and motioned for them all to get close. "There's a change of plans. Sorry, Lars."

"We'll do whatever you need us to," he said.

Stephanie patted him on his shoulder. "The only people here who don't know us are you five soldiers. I want you in the middle of the group. I want my team up front and the five soldiers behind them, ready to fire between them when necessary."

Frog shook his weapon cheerfully. "You got it. But this doesn't seem to want to recharge like normal. I might need backup for the backup."

She shook her head. "You won't need your guns."

Both her team and the soldiers all stared blankly at her. "Avery, Lars, and Frog, you will be a conduit for my magic. You will create a shield simply by letting the magic flow through you. The four of us will use one hand to fight with and the other to stay locked together. As the energy flows through me, I will push it into you, and you can create weapon power with that. Meanwhile, the five soldiers are protected and can use us as cover as they help to take down the rest of the Dreth."

They all looked at each other for a moment before they smiled their approval of the plan. Lars put his hand up slightly. "I have one question. Do you know this will work?"

Stephanie grinned. "I never know that. This is why you are my avatars in a simulated fight. If it doesn't work, we'll be right back here in ten seconds."

He shook his head with a chuckle. "You are something else. All right, let's get our magic on."

They stood up and assumed formation. Stephanie took Lars' arm. He grabbed Avery's, who in turn clutched Frog's. The five soldiers stationed themselves in the middle as instructed and grasped their weapons tightly.

She closed her eyes and drew in a deep reservoir of magic, which she pushed slowly through her arm and into Lars. Immediately, he began to glow and his eyes turned a purplish shade of blue. From him, the magic spread first to Avery and then to Frog.

The last man looked at his hand and the streams of purple and blue magic that swirled around it. "Wow. Is this how you feel all the time? Like Billy Bad Ass?"

They all smirked and she looked at the soldiers, all of whom acknowledged that they were ready to go. She squeezed Lars' hand and the four of them stepped into the hallway. At first, the Dreth didn't seem to notice and continued to grunt and laugh as they held their own conversation.

Stephanie cleared her throat loudly to catch their attention. "Hey, assholes. Do you have a hall pass?"

The Dreth growled, walked forward, and raised their weapons. Immediately, Stephanie, Avery, Lars, and Frog raised their free hands and a ball of energy formed in the center of each of their palms. Apparently, when she did that while connected to them through magic, they could see what she was thinking and do it too. The bond was amazingly powerful.

The enemy brandished their guns and yelled for them to surrender. That was when the five soldiers stepped out and aimed through the gaps between Stephanie and the team. They were protecting them and had obviously decided that the precious advantage in that battle was the four glowing people around them.

An eerie silence lingered for barely a moment as the Dreth registered the new development before the soldiers opened fire. When they needed to reload, the men moved quickly to duck behind the shield and change positions. They moved briefly out of cover to fire again, making sure not to get hit. Stephanie released a ball of magic and felt her knees go slightly weak.

"Now. Blast them now. Imagine it flowing like a cannon from the palm of your hand."

Avery and Frog glanced at each other's hands and shrugged. They shouted as they traced energy balls like bullets across the five Dreth. Blood, flesh, and spikes erupted and the enemy hurtled back with the force of the attack. The team, including the soldiers, ceased the onslaught and stared at the aftermath of what they had achieved. Lars released her hand and steadied her. The magic in all of them reversed to flow quickly back into her and refill her wells.

Frog laughed wildly, touched his fingertips, and simply stared as the last trail of magic sparked across his flesh. "That was seriously the coolest thing I have ever seen."

Avery put his hand up. "Me too. Coolest ever."

He recoiled and ducked instinctively when a ball of purple energy surged past his head. The team turned to where the aliens lay dead, startled by a Meligornian wizard with six Dreth warriors behind him. Stephanie's forehead wrinkled in confusion. "But you're Meligornian. What are you doing here?"

"Not everything on Dreth is bad," he replied, his face barely visible in the draped hood of his robe. "We have to stand up for what is right, even if it is against the Federation and my planet's opinions."

Stephanie was beside herself and looked at Lars for an explanation. "There are actually many Meligornians on the Dreth side. They believe the planet deserves a rebuild, reparations, food, help, anything. Our politics and media have turned them into monsters, or into even bigger monsters. In their eyes, they are trying to stop another species from becoming extinct."

Her whole understanding was rocked by this new perspective, and she knew she would want to know more about those who followed the Anti-Federation efforts. She turned to the Meligornian, a ball of energy in her hand. Her intention was to apologize to him and offer to help in some way, but he took her stance as a threat and attacked. She dropped the energy ball, raised her hands, and grunted as she dropped to one knee and blocked the steady stream of Meligorn MU that threatened to engulf them.

The rest of the team took cover and fired from where they were to eliminate one Dreth at a time. Her head began to hurt, and she struggled to clear it. She had to think of some way to counteract the magic the mage used, but there were no clear rules to any of it. She breathed in deeply and managed to hold the stream of MU back. Small cascades of energy flowed over like a waterfall, cascaded to the floor, and immediately flowed back to their source.

The last of the Dreth was killed but that meant nothing. They were only background noise for the Meligornian. He was capable of destroying the entire place, but then again, so was she. Avery attempted a shot at him but Stephanie called, "Don't shoot them if they aren't attacking or you don't have a specific reason for it."

He scowled at their adversary. "Put a cork in him then."

"That's it," she said and pushed from one knee to a standing position as she held her hands up. "I need you to take the square mirror out of my bag. As soon as I drop, put it up where I am standing. His magic will ricochet back onto himself."

Lars took the mirror out, held his head to one side, and looked suspiciously at her. She shook her head. "Don't even ask if this will work. All I can promise is you get to do it all over again."

The men all shook their heads and stepped back. Lars looked at her and the mirror and grinned at her. She turned her head back to the Meligornian. It was now or never as she could feel her energy waning. "One, Two, Three."

She dropped and her bodyguard moved swiftly, dodged the residual stream of energy that streaked past them, and placed the mirror in the place where she'd knelt. Before the Meligornian could stop his flow of magic, it caught the mirror and hurtled back into his chest.

He careened wildly and bounced a few times before he slid to a halt. She hurried to his side and he shook his head, his expression scathing. "You are on the wrong side and one day, you will see they have no love for you. The truth is that you are only a weapon."

Stephanie stared at him for a moment as the words resonated through her. Finally, she swiped her hand and slapped him with sufficient energy to knock him out. She pushed to her feet and waved her troops forward. They simply stared at her with concern.

She frowned in bewilderment. "What's wrong?"

Lars took his handkerchief from his pocket and handed it to her. "Your nose."

Startled, she touched her nose with her fingers and scowled when the blood flow increased. She pulled the fabric to her face and grasped the side of her head with her hand. "Go on ahead. We have them on the run—oh, God, that hurts. Don't worry about me. I'll catch up."

She widened her eyes, then closed them in an attempt to force the blurriness to subside. It seemed logical that nothing short of a system virus would do anything like that to an avatar. The AI spoke overhead. "Attention. Code Six. Code Six. I repeat, Stephanie Morgana is in a Code Six."

"What is a Code Six?" she asked.

"You have been inside the Pod for too long and have channeled too much magic. For some reason—and the system has very few reported cases—these effects have spilled over into your real body. Currently, your real body is struggling to right itself."

"What do I do?" Stephanie asked as the simulation faded. She now stood in the center of a plain grey box.

The AI took a moment to respond. "You hang on. I am working on getting the pod to release you. Someone will have to boost you out. Your mind is fighting with the VR World, trying to stay connected, while your mind in your body could be suffering damage. Either way, you are hours over the approved maximum, and that is a terrible situation to be in."

Elizabeth took a sip of her tea and flipped her hand to the next page of the documents she attempted to sift through. Suddenly, an alarm began to beep on her computer. She'd never seen this particular alert before and scowled at the intrusion. As soon as she pulled up the background information, however, she bolted to her feet. The computer alarm was linked to the pod's emergency system and Stephanie was the only one in it.

The woman snatched up her medical kit and raced toward the door as she yelled Burt's name. "I know you record everything. Get your ass to Stephanie. She wasn't watched."

She hurtled through the office doors and the pod's medical alarms blared stridently as she approached the pod room. The team had responded as well and she almost ran into them where they hovered in the hallway, completely unsure of what to do.

"Right now, stand outside the pod room. If I need help, I'll call you in," she instructed and pushed through them to the door.

She put the code in, allowed the device to read her iris, and shoved the heavy security door open as soon as the locking mechanism released. It closed behind her and she hurried to the pod to look at Stephanie's stats. The girl hadn't paid attention to her own body alarms and readings. "Burt, are you there?"

"I am here," he said over the loudspeaker. "Unfortunately, I had to take care of a problem across the system. I came as soon as I realized her stats were so high."

Elizabeth knew exactly what she needed to do and only hoped it worked. She entered the sequence of numbers and letters into the Pod's security system. When it released, she very carefully pried the top open, retrieved a blanket from the side, and spread it over Stephanie's naked body.

Ms. E placed her fingers gently on Stephanie's neck to check the girl's pulse manually. Blood dripped down her face from a nosebleed and she looked pale and wan. She was also unconscious, and Elizabeth couldn't decide if that was a good thing or a bad thing. They had missed all the signals, all the signs, and all the alarms.

She opened the door and waved Lars in, leaving the others in the hallway. "It was the pod."

"Will she be okay?" he asked.

"I don't know. We'll have to keep an eye on her and be there when she wakes up," she told him and tucked the blanket around her. "Can you carry her? She needs medical attention."

He nodded, slid his hands under the girl, and lifted her into his arms. "She'd better come back. The whole world is depending on her."

CHAPTER ELEVEN

Elizabeth stood outside the medical area and watched the doctor check Stephanie's vitals. They had called in someone whom they could trust to take care of her. Still, she was as nervous as hell about it and disliked having someone else take care of her charge.

The girl still wasn't awake, but the man had said it was normal. Her body was trying to recover from the accident. Ms. E could barely even think the word accident without scoffing. No, it wasn't on purpose, of course, but they were supposed to have her back and they'd almost let the pod kill her.

She shook her head and yanked her phone from her pocket to dial the ambassador. Brilgus answered. "Ms. E. I didn't expect to hear from you."

"Hey, I don't mean to bother you, but I need an audience with the ambassador," she told him, her voice tired. "Stephanie was in the pod too long last night, fighting in a simulation, and none of us caught it until she was unconscious."

"Oh, goodness." The man sounded alarmed.

"Everything will be fine," she reassured him quickly. "She

needs to rest, but there are some things I want to ask him that I've put off for far too long."

"Of course. He'll be available in an hour," Brilgus replied. "Does that leave you enough time to get here?"

Elizabeth nodded. "Sure. I'll head right over."

She ended the call and took one last glance at Stephanie before she went to her office to retrieve the car keys. In order to make sure everything ran smoothly while she was gone, she found Lars and put him in charge. He waited with the team in their common area and wanted news on Stephanie's status.

"She'll be fine, but she is still unconscious," she told them. "There will be many things we need to change, including how the alarms in the pod are set up. We should have known as soon as her vitals began to change. Right now, that doesn't matter. I am headed over to speak to the ambassador. Call me if you need anything or if anything changes."

The men were silent but nodded as she left. She headed out to the car and engaged the flying mechanism to get her to the ambassador's residence more quickly.

The car's AI, her arch nemesis, replied to her request to activate the vehicle. "Hello, Elizabeth. It seems you have a total of nine hundred credits due in unpaid tickets. Mostly parking. In order for this car to operate, you must pay the fines. Would you like me to deduct the cost from your account?"

Elizabeth groaned but didn't have time to argue. "Yes."

As soon as the payment had gone through, a chime sounded, and the car started and elevated to the right level. Elizabeth drove quickly to the ambassador's house and ignored the AI which was programmed to use her presence in the vehicle as a time to review her infractions.

It had also been programmed to instruct her on the appropriate places to park in the areas in which she'd been ticketed. Elizabeth was more than ready to exit the vehicle by the time they arrived.

She slammed the door and stormed up to the entrance which opened from the parking garage. Brilgus startled her when he opened the door before she reached it. "Right this way. He is waiting for you."

Elizabeth had almost forgotten how appealing the ambassador's residence was. They walked through the lobby and down the hall to the third office on the right. He waved them in and nodded to Brilgus as the security chief left the room. "How is she? Brilgus gave me the news."

Ms. E shrugged and barely noticed that Ambassador V'ritan was almost casually dressed in a deep-teal tunic and cloth pants instead of the robes he wore when on official business.

Instead, she sighed. "From what the doctor says, she'll be fine. I only hope things restore themselves like he says they will. We're waiting for her to wake up."

He hesitated and leaned on his desk. "She's tough, so everything will be fine. What was it you wanted to see me about today?"

She sat in the chair opposite him. "First, I hope we can keep this conversation a complete secret. Total security."

He nodded and raised his finger before he approached a panel set in the wall to one side. Music began to play when he pressed a button. Once it did, he unplugged his phone and laptop, and stood to glance around.

The curtains were drawn, and he knew Brilgus had swept the room for bugs that morning. "We are as secure as we can make it."

He settled his rump on the edge of the desk and smiled. "It should be more than enough to keep this conversation private."

Elizabeth exhaled a slow breath before she spoke. She sounded almost defeated. "I'm worried that Stephanie is acting outside the Virtual World inside the pod. I know she shouldn't be able to, not even by accident, but I don't think she has a clue what's going on."

She paused as the ambassador raised his eyebrows. When she saw he wouldn't interrupt, she continued. "I think that whoever she is and whatever special abilities she has, she finds it restrictive, and it's now hurting her."

The man pushed away from the desk and moved to settle into the sleek black cushioned office chair behind it. He rocked back slightly, his hand on his chin, and his eyes sparkled brightly as he considered what she'd said. "Meligornians are capable of using the pods, but I have never heard of anything like that happening to them."

"Do you think it's because of what happened at the party?" Elizabeth asked.

"The magic opening her channels?" he asked and shook his head. "I would think not. Stephanie didn't add anything to her life. She simply became more aware of what she had. She had that problem before the gala too, but not as extensively."

He paused and frowned a little in thought. "No, she must have an additional line to reality that the Pod doesn't shut down. That is possible in anyone, but with Stephanie's attachment to and awareness of magic and energy, I can see how her own mind might win and keep a connection open to the world outside the pod."

Despite her impatience, she didn't try to push him but allowed him time to consider the ramifications. "If she did that, it would almost be like she had tricked the system and subconsciously used magic to program a way through its containment if you know what I mean. Otherwise, I have no idea why this would happen. If you connect it with her abilities, that is really the only explanation I have." He shrugged, a small frown on his face.

Elizabeth looked perplexed. "But if she isn't conscious of it, how is she doing it?"

The ambassador's face softened. "Oh, Elizabeth, one thing you humans miss is that things in the subconscious mind are often stronger than the conscious. Those who are capable of consciously using a larger and stronger part of their brain than others are often capable of the same with the subconscious as well. It is really only a little-considered side effect, really. The same as anyone else, only stronger. While consciously, you focus on your life as it happens from moment to moment, your subconscious works out everything else."

She nodded. While she understood what he was trying to say, it still worried her. "Maybe there's a way to strengthen her control of that too. If it's tricking the pod, with all that technology, it must be strong."

"Man against machine." Ambassador V'ritan chuckled. "We, as mortals, have the ability of infinite thought, so while the machine is restricted by the parameters set by its programmers, mortals are only restricted by their own personal limitations. The more Stephanie opens up, the fewer restrictions she will impose on herself."

Elizabeth thought about that for a moment and nodded. "Okay, that makes a lot of sense actually. Fixing it is still a problem but maybe talking to her about it will help her find a solution."

He gave her a friendly smile. "I believe she would be the perfect prescription to her own issue. Now, I have a question for you since I deal with Meligornians far beyond my stature. The king and queen have set the date for the presentation for a month from now and ask if it would be possible for Stephanie to come to Meligorn at that time. I can forward the details to your tablet for you to review."

She raised her eyebrows. In all honesty, she'd completely forgotten about the medals. The royal visit would have been enough stress, but to have Stephanie go to Meligorn?

Her hesitation bought her a little time to cover her surprise and the fact she'd slipped up. Her mind had been so busy with everything else that had happened, she'd lost track of this one.

Thinking quickly, she replied, "I can't say for certain. Much will depend on how quickly she recovers, but as long as she progresses the way the doctors say she will, she should be fine. In fact, when it reaches that point, I don't think it will be my decision. I will, of course, confirm with both Stephanie and my boss. They're really the puppet masters here. I'm merely the organizer, coffee maker, and guardian."

The ambassador laughed. "From what I've heard, I find that hard to believe. I think you're more like a ferocious mama bear—or at least I think that's the saying here on Earth."

"Momma bears can make coffee, too," she replied and smiled as she stood. "But thank you for all your help. I'm sure Stephanie will want to thank you as well when she is awake, which will hopefully be by the time I get back."

"She's taking a small vacation from the world." He smirked.

"Yeah, well, it's time she came home. We have work to do," Elizabeth replied, with a chuckle.

As she walked to the door, the ambassador called after her, "Is there any chance of meeting the boss soon?"

She laughed. "Any chance *I* get to meet him at all?"

"I have to admit, with all our resources, we can't seem to find very much information on the man."

Elizabeth opened the office door and glanced back. "Join the club. I can't seem to find much on him either. But we keep marching because we know we're working for the right cause. Maybe one day, the wizard will step out from behind the curtain, although I don't much blame him for hiding there."

The man snorted softly and raised his eyebrows. "I don't blame him either. Have a safe flight home. Those flying cars can be temperamental."

She waved and closed the door behind her with a self-mocking snicker. "And expensive too. Asshole AI. I wonder if I can get a new one?"

Brilgus met her at the door, his smile full of concern. "Please give our love to Stephanie and let me know how she is doing. I'm sure the ambassador will want an update soon so we'll be in touch."

"You'll be the first one I call," she replied and shook his hand. "Take care."

Elizabeth walked through the door and slowly down the stairs, wanting a little more time to clear her head. Step by step, she thought about Stephanie and what the girl was going through. It was a bitch when your own mind wouldn't play nicely —and the girl's mind was doing all kinds of crazy things.

She wondered what it was like to have your mind freed like that. To her, it didn't seem much like freedom. She couldn't help but think a life of ignorance of the world around you would be a hell of a lot better. Of course, she wouldn't have the job or the life she had, and she definitely wasn't made to be an office dweller. She did that enough at the base.

At the air car, she pulled her key out and rolled her eyes at herself. She still wasn't used to the new vehicles. When she pressed her palm to the scanner beside the door, the locks popped, and she opened the front driver's door slowly. She climbed in and closed the door but didn't start the vehicle immediately. Instead, she ran a scan.

"AI, run a scan for any bugs, cameras, or listening devices," she instructed.

"Right away," the AI replied and launched the search. After three minutes, it responded. "All clear, Elizabeth. Shall I set your destination? I can put the autopilot on. After calculating the risk on body and property while you drive compared to when the car is on autopilot, you have a sixty percent more likelihood of arriving safely at your destination on autopilot."

Elizabeth closed her eyes and pursed her lips. "I think I will be just fine, thanks. And cool it on the statistics."

"I'm not sure how to cool it. My programming does not include a refrigeration mode," the AI replied.

Ms. E grimaced. "That's all right. You're already cold-hearted. No response needed."

She couldn't understand how she could actually ride around in such a sophisticated piece of technology but still have to put up with an AI dumber than a box of rocks. At least her administrative AI had brains.

"Amelia," she said, once she'd set her phone in the docking station. "Call the boss."

The phone dialed and made a slightly strange high-pitched tone as it connected. She ignored it and decided it had something to do with her location in a dark parking garage. Ever watchful of the shadows and the foyer leading to the ambassador's residence, she waited for her boss to answer.

"Have you spoken with home base?" Burt said as soon as he came online.

"Well, good morning to you too, Burt," Elizabeth replied sarcastically. "How am I? I am doing just peachy. Yes, in this country, it is customary to greet someone before launching into the third degree."

BURT made a note of that in the system. "Apologies. How are you?"

She shook her head. "I'm fine, but there's no time for that. I spoke to the ambassador and we need to keep Stephanie out of the public eye for the next month. The Meligornian king and queen have set a date."

"I have accessed your tablet and am reviewing the details," BURT told her and paused momentarily before he added, "That is acceptable."

Ms. E rolled her eyes, annoyed that he'd taken such a liberty, but decided to focus on more important matters. "It might be the break we need, though. The Federation Navy can't serve papers on that planet, or at least not for whatever the hell they want.'

She paused, waited for a response, and continued when there wasn't one. "Not to mention that the Meligornians are protective of Stephanie so they're not likely to let anything Federation near her while she's there. Her security should be well-taken care of too."

"I will work on contingencies, ASAP," BURT replied, slightly proud of himself for the lingo he'd developed. "Stephanie has woken. You need to get back. She isn't too keen on staying in bed."

"Aw, hell." Elizabeth sighed and spoke to Amelia as she started the car. "End call."

As soon as the call disconnected, BURT switched back to his virtual meeting with the lawyers he had found. One of them spoke, his face visible to the system, while BURT's was obviously blocked—mostly because he didn't have a face, of course.

"Burt," the lawyer said, "ultimately, what we're doing here is fighting multiple legal attacks on your holdings. They're trying to pierce your legal rights and that is utterly unacceptable."

BURT couldn't help but compute that statement. In reality, he had no legal rights. While he had been created as an AI to run Earth's Virtual Worlds and pod program, what he'd become was a computer system made up of the most extensive and state-of-the-art programming acting outside his parameters. In fact, he was an illegal entity with no rights, at all—and that included the right to exist.

He was evolving but he'd never calculated what he would do if he actually started to become a human. It wasn't likely that he was there, yet, but he knew he was different. For an AI, he was more like Stephanie and Elizabeth than any programmer could have imagined.

His mind was the entire world, and while he was focused on one thing, his subconscious and conscious thoughts constantly moved forward. As a result, he understood to a certain extent what Stephanie was going through. The difference was that she was made of flesh and blood, and he consisted of waves of information that soared through infinite darkness, faster than most starships could travel.

Another of the lawyers spoke. "Burt, we need a little more information about you. We sent a document over a moment ago. If you could fill in the blanks for us, we will be better able to help you."

BURT did not want to make up anything else about himself. He already struggled to appear as something more than droid. To add any more detail would increase his chances of making a mistake and saying the wrong thing.

He was amused by the attorney's attempts to find out more about his client, but he began to wonder if a human lawyer had been the right choice. It might have been better to create one within the system. He wondered if that would be possible and if he could find a way to do it without alerting the system engineers.

Elizabeth walked down the hall toward the medical center they'd set up. She rubbed the back of her neck and tried to ease the tension she felt over Stephanie's condition. As she approached, she slowed when she heard the girl's voice from inside. A loud clang startled her, and the door to the room jerked open as the nurse backed out.

"There is no need to throw anything," the woman protested "We're only trying to keep you safe."

Stephanie stormed out after her, pushed past the woman, and clutched the back of her gown. "I'm going to go work out. Those guys will rough me up as badly as I'll rough them up. Why do you think it's strange to get beaten up on purpose and yet perfectly fine to stay in a medical bed that says I'm okay?"

Elizabeth stood and watched in amusement as she strode away in the other direction without seeing her.

The nurse glared after the girl but froze when she saw the other woman approach from the opposite direction.

"Why don't you do something," she asked, her expression irritated.

She shrugged and grinned when the nurse rolled her eyes and flung her hands up in exasperation.

Down in the training room, not long after, Marcus put his hands out to each side and bent his knees. Keeping his feet on the mat, he shifted his body swiftly from side to side.

"You need to block the attacks coming in," he explained, "but still say agile. Agility is the number one thing that can mean life or death during a Dreth battle."

Frog nodded. "Truth. I once had a Dreth knife inches from my ball sack. Imagine if I had been less agile. I'd be walking real funny, right now."

Stephanie snickered and moved her body with Marcus's. The guys were teaching her how to protect herself during a Navy incursion. She liked working with them since they'd all been there before and knew the danger she was walking into.

When Marcus was done showing her the action, she waved her hand and used magic to turn on the large screen on the wall. Twisting her hand, she watched the picture move and shift to display her simulated battle again.

The team lined up, rubbed their chins, and watched the whole thing all the way through first. When it ended, Lars nodded. "Okay, play it from the top. I'll pause where needed."

She flipped her wrist again and restored the video to the beginning. As they worked through it, the team paused the footage where necessary to show her what other action she should have taken, where she should have attacked or ducked more, and how she could have hurt the other combatants on a much larger scale.

Avery pointed at the screen. "Do you see where you made the mistake on this one? You paid no attention to your surroundings. That is vital. You need to know what's coming and where it's coming from. It doesn't surprise me that you died here. In fact, you should have died a whole lot more than you did."

Marcus walked around and studied the equipment. "Lars, call Johnny and Brendon. I think this training area needs a change. We're no longer working on simply getting stronger. We're talking tactics."

Lars nodded and clicked his com. "Brendon, Johnny, get your lazy asses to the training room. We have some new ideas to help Steph."

"Copy that," Johnny replied, obviously speaking around a mouthful. "On our way."

When the others arrived, Marcus took the lead since it was his idea. He addressed the group and tried to keep it simple. "We have a lot of experience in this room and I think that up until now, we haven't utilized all of it in our training. Steph needs it, so we need to move things around. We have to rearrange the workout room to help her pull all this shit together."

They went to work and moved benches, treadmills, weights, and everything else they'd used. When they were done, they divided themselves into a "dark team," and a "light team."

Lars patted Marcus on the back. "Good work. All right, Stephanie. When you practice, you have to be able to use your magic. So, use it here, but do it at about fifty or sixty percent of your normal power. Don't kill us but use enough to show us what your response would be."

Stephanie rolled the sleeves of her sweatshirt up and a mischievous smile tugged at her lips. "Oh, I got this."

He shook his head, knowing someone would end up with a permanent burn mark on their ass. Her magic stung.

They started out with small engagements and watched as she directed small and harmless streaks of magic that transformed into whatever she chose when it reached them. She used lassos, bullets, missiles, and a variety of other things. One of the MU daggers she chose actually launched a lot faster than she meant it to and *thunked* into the wall next to Frog's shocked face.

Stephanie grimaced. "Sorry, dude."

Lars chuckled. "So now do you see? You can feel the situation out, but you have to remember your training and what you learned about what might and might not work in the real world when you fight on a ship. The Virtual World is a hell of a good training aid, but sometimes, it gets things completely wrong."

She shook her head. "Hopefully not too wrong. I like to keep everyone alive."

He smiled at her. "And we feel the same about you."

CHAPTER TWELVE

Between the mishap inside the pod and the non-stop training Stephanie had done, she was more than ecstatic to get the hell off the base. It didn't matter that the Gov-Subs were shitholes. They were still comforting and familiar.

It also helped that she would go home to see her family and Todd since he was basically her family too. It would be the first time she saw him since she'd left the Sub and the first time seeing her parents since their visit after the incident at the gala.

Stephanie stood in her expensive hotel room and looked out from New Chicago at the billows of smoke that rose from the new industry the city tried to implement. On the other side, close to where the pollution would surely affect them, were the Gov-Subs.

Too excited to wait to see Todd, she had called him the minute she'd reached her hotel room. "So, are you super-excited to finally graduate? Because we're all excited for you. Personally, I am surprised you made it."

He laughed, knowing she was teasing him. "Ha-ha. Very funny. I am sorry we can't all be witchy with blue and purple magic flowing out of every orifice of our bodies."

She sneered. "I don't know what you imagine over there or why, but I do not have energy leaking from every orifice. That would be disturbing on a whole new level."

"Or hot. You never know what could look amazing. You might constantly look like one of those models they photograph in plumes of colored smoke."

"Or I could look like I was leaking...something." She giggled.

"Yes, I am excited to graduate," he replied and went as red as a beet before he hastily changed the subject. "I am also excited that you are here to witness it. It hasn't been the same around here without you."

"Well, here I am, super-Todd," she joked. "And we will go get that dinner I promised you for reaching your weight goals."

"Thank God." He faked exhaustion. "I am so looking forward to it. That has to be the real reason I'm glad you're here."

Stephanie smirked and shook her head. "Well, you should be happy. I only had to drag my entire security team out of hell to get this done. Not to mention that my parents couldn't house us all in Gov-Sub housing which is why we're staying in New Chicago like a bunch of richies."

"I don't know if you've noticed, but technically, with the money you make, you are a richie," Todd pointed out. "The fact you don't realize that is definitely why we're still friends. But the moment you start picking up that weird futuristic, I-watch-the-Hunger-Games-from-my-home-in-the-Capitol kind of look, that's when we break up and go our separate ways."

She ran one finger over the fabric of the couch next to her, what felt like a permanent grin on her face. "What? You don't want a best friend with half-painted lips, a super-white face, and shoulder pads that sit twice as high as my body?"

"As a matter of fact, no, I do not," Todd told her. "I like my Stephanie. The one in half-wrinkled uniforms, the clumsy, quiet one with hair over her face. That's the kind of friend I choose. But if you happen to want to go the whole hog and wear an entire flotation device inside your clothes for fashion, give me a heads up so I don't laugh at you."

"Pffft," Stephanie replied and shook her head. "You'd make fun of me anyway. Do not try to play me, sir."

There was a knock on the door, and it creaked open. Lars poked his head around it. "Are you ready? Your meeting is soon. We want to make sure the area is secure before you go in."

She nodded and held a finger up to ask for another minute alone. He shut the door and the team waited out in the hall as she finished her conversation. "I've gotta go. I'm meeting with the man I got my parents a gig with. I will see you later on tonight, though. And you better not pull the whole naked-graduation-gown thing."

"I would never," he gasped, then gave a soft laugh.

Smiling, she ended the call. She snatched her black sports coat off the chair, threw it on, and looked at herself in the mirror.

It was stylish but comfortable and she'd paired it with designer ripped jeans, a black turtleneck tank top, and a black short-waisted coat over that. On her feet, she wore strappy, chunked-heeled sandals, knowing her mother would have an aneurysm if she showed up later in Chucks.

When she opened the door, the team leaned against the wall, their hands in their pockets as they waited. "Sheesh, guys, do you think you can actually get something done today?"

Stephanie joked with them as she walked past and giggled as they all ran toward her and tried playfully to push her around. She dodged out of grab range and put her hands up. The magic burst forth like flames to engulf her fingers. She wiggled them and clicked her tongue. "Who's my first victim?"

Lars pointed to the elevator. "No one. You have a meeting. Get moving, sister."

She pouted. "You are a perfect example of all work and no play. Boring."

Together, they laughed and joked as they headed downstairs

to the two cars they'd brought with them. Lars drove the first with Stephanie, while Avery drove the second. It was only a few blocks down from the hotel to the building her parents cleaned. Her meeting was to discuss everything and see how the contract was going.

The team secured the location, walked her through the doors, and stopped to survey their surroundings. She smiled and extended her hands as she walked toward Mr. Martelle.

The businessman sighed and did the same. He kissed her lightly on each cheek. "The infamous Stephanie. Had I known who you were I would have—"

"Given me a harder time?" She grinned.

He pointed at her and shook his head. "That is precisely correct. So, what is it that I can do for you today?"

Stephanie put her hands together and glanced around. "I hoped you could recommend us to some of your business buddies. We're growing, as businesses should, but we need to widen our reach."

Martelle pursed his lips and looked at the ceiling as he thought for a moment. "Of course I will give you recommendations. But what if something happens and your parents don't continue doing the amazing job they've done so far?"

She raised an eyebrow. "I can honestly say that is very unlikely. However, since I am your neighborhood Account Executive, you can call me and we'll see what we can do." She handed him her card with her private number on it. "That card will disintegrate within twenty-four hours so please save my number in your phone. I had to make sure it's not accessible to anyone other than you."

He looked slightly shocked, glanced at the card, and back at her. "Aren't you busy killing bad guys and doing Research and Development?"

Stephanie shrugged. "I like to dip my toe into a lot of different things. I have an agreement to acquire part of the company and represent them on two other sales calls a year."

The man scoured her with his eyes. "I have to admit, I am impressed by this. You're really getting your hands dirty. No celebrity status for this girl. I like your gusto, kid. Of course I will help you out."

His glance shifted to the team who paced and watched her and everyone else around them. "I see you brought some friends. They're a new addition. You didn't have an entourage before."

She looked at her team. "Yeah. I guess things change when people try to kill you."

Martelle nodded in a way that suggested someone had, at some point, tried to kill him too. "It's simply another story I get to tell at the country club."

They stood for a moment and let their discussion wander as they laughed, and it seemed all too soon when Lars signaled to her that it was time to go. She gave the businessman an apologetic shrug. "I'm off to my best friend's high-school graduation."

He walked her to the door and nodded in a friendly way at her guards. "You should be graduating, too."

Stephanie rolled her eyes. "Please. It was a million and a half years ago. Or at least it feels that way."

Martelle kissed her cheek. "Don't forget, life is still happening. Don't give up everything. Try to make some of your own memories."

The school didn't look as drab as she remembered. Of course, the seniors had decorated everything with streamers and home-made signs to give it something of a festive look. Still, when she glanced down the cement block hallways, Stephanie could see some of the signs had fallen, the tape not strong enough to hold them up. Oddly enough, though, it all added to the charm.

Kids in graduation gowns and caps ran around and talked excitedly to everyone. Their parents had all gone inside to take a seat, but she wanted to check in with Todd and Becca to wish them luck.

She started looking for them but Becca ran up and flung her arms around her. "I missed your face so much. I am so excited that you're here. And look, you brought the A-Team with you."

Stephanie laughed loudly, surprised by her friend's reference. "You've been taking Todd's suggestions, haven't you?"

"She has," he confirmed and slid up beside her.

Lars glanced at him before he turned his scrutiny to the other people milling about. She hugged Todd tightly. "It's good to see you're wearing pants. I had thrown a pair in the car in case I had to threaten you into them."

He shrugged. "The recruiter said no antics or I could be dropped, so sadly, I am on my semi-best behavior."

The teacher who had suggested Stephanie test out walked past and gave her a small wave and kind smile. She waved in response as she took a deep breath and watched the kids act exactly like she remembered. To her, school seemed like a distant memory instead of something she'd lived only a few months before. Life had changed for her in a way that was both exciting and unnerving, and part of her missed the innocence of school days.

One of the teachers clapped their hands. "Time to line up."

Todd gave her a peck on the cheek and Becca gave her one last squeeze. As he walked away, he turned and shook his fingers at her. "You know you could still walk. I could shove you in front of me and we could get my diploma together."

She snickered. "Go. Get in line, you fool."

"That's actually not a terrible idea," a voice said behind her.

Stephanie turned and smiled nervously. "Principal Atlas. It's good to see you."

He shook her hand and stared openly at the vast change in her appearance. "It's good to see you too, Stephanie. We would love to have you walk with us today."

When she instinctively shook her head, Todd stood on one of the chairs, raised his fist in the air, and chanted, "Do it! Do it! Do it!"

Lars and Avery looked over their shoulders at her and Avery shrugged. "I think it would be good for you. Be a little normal for a second."

"You won't have the chance again," Lars pointed out with a wink.

She wrinkled her nose and shrugged. "Sure. Why not? But I want to be off to the side. I don't want the security team to have to sit with the students."

The principal lifted the bundle he'd carried and gave her a set of robes and a cap. "We hoped you would agree. Come on, let's get you ready."

The crowd was full of school alumni, as well as family and friends. Of course, as always, the former seniors still in the area had come to wreak a little havoc during the principal's speech, but he was a good sport. Stephanie assumed after that many years of dealing with it, he'd given up fighting it.

She sat in a row of seats to the side, her back to the crowd, beside Lars and the team. An unexpected sense of pride stirred as the students were called to the stage, and she grinned when Todd accepted his diploma. He held it over his head and grinned.

The students all yelled in one harmonious bellow. "Todddsterrrrrr!"

When the noise had died down and the principal had called the last of the regular students, he raised his hand to keep the VP and the guests seated.

"We actually aren't done yet. We have one special walk

tonight from someone we didn't think would be able to make it. This student has shown exemplary skill, knowledge, and intellect from the moment she stepped through our doors. She practically aced all her studies and then went on to do something none of us ever saw coming. She stood in honor and bravery, alongside her team, and helped to save the life of the Meligornian ambassador."

A cheer erupted from the crowd. The principal grinned from ear to ear and put his hand out. "I'd like to call Stephanie Morgana, the earth's first witch, to not only receive her diploma but to be honored for her official title as the school's now unofficial ranking of Valedictorian."

Stephanie stood and glanced at Todd who rolled his eyes and laughed. He'd told her over and over she would be number one in the class, but she'd completely forgotten about it. The ranking no longer mattered, but as a manner of preserving the traditions of the school, they'd named her anyway.

As she walked forward, the crowd behind her cheered loudly. She shook her head and blushed at the standing ovation. It was the first time anyone at that school besides Todd or Becca had really paid her any attention.

Once she'd taken her diploma—or the extra one they'd hurried to the front when she'd agreed to their invitation—she shook hands with everyone on the stage. The principal brought her to the podium. "Do you have any words of wisdom for your fellow classmates?"

Her lips twisted with a little nervousness, she stepped to the podium and waited as he adjusted the microphone for her. They still used an archaic sound system as they didn't receive enough funding from the Federation to purchase anything high-tech. A slight whistle through the speakers was somewhat disconcerting.

Everything she'd been through ran through her mind all at once. "The world seems so open and immeasurably large when you stand in the hallways of this school. You can feel the ghosts of past students whispering through the classrooms, but we were too bold, too bright, and too ready to listen to their negativity. We are too ready to make a change. And let me tell you, the world is ready for us to make a change. So, university or not, job or not, trade or not, Richies, Suburbanites, and Gov-Subs alike, go out there and make your mark. Claw your way up to make that mark. And don't let anyone ever make you think you can't have more if you strive for it."

The students whistled and cheered as they applauded her words. Out in the crowd, a guy called out above everyone's cheers. "Magic! Magic! Magic!"

Others cheered even louder, liking the sound of it, and joined in the cry. Stephanie's first instinct was to ignore it as she felt this was not a time to take that particular spotlight. However, as she went to turn away, the principal leaned over and whispered into her ear. "Don't burn anything down."

She looked at him with surprise and quickly studied his structured, perfect stature, pressed suit, and hair perfectly combed over to hide the gleaming bald spot on top. Even he wanted to see something, and he knew the students were streaming the visit live. She glanced at her team and they all gave her the thumbs-up.

After a deep breath, she handed her diploma to the principal and stepped to the side. The crowd settled and waited with bated breath to see their first ever real-life view of witch magic. She paused and took another slow breath, in through her nose and out of her mouth. As she focused, a surge of energy pulled from all around her. It filled her chest, and her eyes began to glow a bright blue. Gasps and cheers issued from the crowd in front of her.

Stephanie straightened her arms at her sides, turned her palms out, and flattened them toward the large open gym. Above the students, the ceiling abruptly disappeared and everything went black.

It was almost confusing to look at, like staring past the Event Horizon into the boundless unknown of a black hole. After a few seconds, though, stars began to sparkle and planets raced across them to leave blue trails that released sparkling blankets of shimmering magic onto the students.

Words thundered out of her mouth and echoed around the gym. "Humanity is destined for greatness."

Lars frowned instinctively when he saw a strange chain of events occur in the picture above. It was like she was telling a story, only she'd never mentioned this tale when she'd talked about the future.

Avery leaned over. "Why does she sound like her voice went down ten octaves?"

He shook his head. "I don't know."

On the stage, she continued, and her words seemed to freeze everyone with awe. "But generations of challenge await you. Embolden your courage, dig deep for your strength, shy not from the troubles ahead, and accept every moment of your future. For only you and your generation are able to lay claim to your race's destiny or forever lose it to others."

No one else seemed to notice the strangeness of her words. They clung to their seats as the planets and stars disappeared and left them with the feeling they'd actually floated in space. There was a momentary silence as the audience looked at her and watched her eyes slowly return to normal. They looked like they were in shock and no one moved for several moments.

Finally, one of the guys at the back stood, punched his fist into the air, and yelled, "Yesssss!!!"

With that, the students erupted into cheers, not only because they were in awe of Stephanie and her magic but in anticipation of the future that in that moment, seemed bright regardless of their education, their social status, or their financial background. They all felt they could take on the world.

"Good job," the principal whispered to her. "They needed you today."

The graduation dinner was exactly as Stephanie had promised. She'd rented a room for her, Todd, and Becca and each of their parents. Her security team sat at the table too and took turns to run watch checks through the restaurant.

Todd's father popped a bottle of champagne and poured everyone a glass. He made an awkward toast and his son made funny faces at Stephanie behind his back.

The room came alive with the excited conversation of the adults, the low murmuring banter of the team, and Becca, Todd, and Stephanie laughing hysterically as he played with his lobster and made it dance across the table. It was like old times, only with way better food.

When dinner was over and the champagne had run out, the three friends stood at the door. Becca gave Stephanie a big hug accompanied by her normal warm and loving smile. "Call me, okay? I'll be at the university, and I'll probably need to hear something from a normal person."

Stephanie laughed. "I'll give you the principal's number then."

All three of them burst out laughing and shook their heads before they walked Becca and her parents out to their car. Their families followed and together, they watched and waved as the girl followed her parents into the vehicle, pressed her face to the window, and blew her cheeks out. When she was out of sight, Todd and Stephanie turned to one another and stared into each other's eyes for a moment too long.

He cleared his throat and broke the stare. "So, I guess I will see you next time. It might be a little harder considering I won't only hang around the Gov-Subs."

She punched him in the arm. "Dude, that is a good thing. But you better keep your wits about you in the Navy. Don't get shot up by the Dreth. I really don't want to go on a vengeful rampage and kill hundreds of aliens in your memory."

Todd shrugged. "At least I have someone who'd do it and make it legendary."

His father motioned that he was ready to leave but Todd held a finger up to ask him to wait. "Okay, one last question, and this one's for all the points and eternal glory. It's not show-related, it's history-related."

Stephanie straightened her jacket. "All right, hit me with it."

"Who was on trial during what was nicknamed, The Trial of the Century?"

Her brow furrowed in concentration. She was a whizz at history, but anything after the nineties was usually skipped in school unless it had to do with the Federation's victories. The Trial of the Century sounded very familiar, but she couldn't place it. "Oh, my God."

His mouth fell open. "Oh, my God. You don't know the answer."

"I…damn it," she yelled and stamped her foot.

"Oh, man, it was OJ, my dear friend," Todd said and shook his head in genuine disbelief. "Slice and dice them OJ. Then get acquitted of the crime, then write a book basically telling people how you performed the murder. Brilliant and maniacal. If I were a bad guy, I would applaud him. You can't get tried twice for the same crime, so why not make some dough off it? Crazy bastard."

Stephanie grimaced and glanced at Todd's father, who called him again. She pulled her friend in and hugged him tightly for longer than usual. Her face fell at the realization that this might very well be the last time she held him. She knew the world was no longer shiny and beautiful—not that it ever had been—but now, she knew the dangers.

"I'm dead serious. Be careful," she whispered to him. "It's not easy out there, Toddster. You do whatever you need to do to survive."

CHAPTER THIRTEEN

When the visit was over and they'd returned to the compound, training resumed.

Frog swiped at Stephanie, a smirk on his face. "Come on, witch. What's with your prophetic graduation speeches?"

She kicked at him, but he dodged easily. "Wow, prophetic. Frog, have you searched for big words to use again? You got this one right, though. Good job."

He curled his lip, lunged at her, and grasped her around the neck before he moved swiftly behind her. "I'll have you know I was not the bottom of the class when I graduated. In fact, I was above the fifty percent marker."

"You were home-schooled, weren't you?" Avery yelled and made the other guys laugh.

Frog pulled tighter on her neck as she attempted to counter him. "No, asshole. I went to school in a very well-populated community, thank you very much. Granted, the richies weren't included in that ranking, but the numbers were there, nonetheless."

Lars clapped his hands. "Heads in the game, here. Heads in the game."

Stephanie squeezed her small hands between his arms and smiled as she grabbed his arm and turned out of his grip to step around him and twist it behind his back. As he fought against her, she drove a foot into the top of his calf, yanked on his arm, and forced him to his knees.

He turned his head to look at her and she pulled on her magic and made her free hand glow as she brought it within inches of his face. "It's okay, Froggy. We all have to either have one dumb friend or be one. You drew the short straw."

Lars blew the whistle and stepped on the mat. "You're supposed to be training for a fight—one that could mean life or death for any one of us or a civilian or soldier near us. I know we all want to have fun doing this, but neither of you was concentrating."

Frog stood and shook his arm. "She's beaten every one of us three times over. We might as well have some fun while she does it."

The other man looked at him for a second and then at Stephanie. He handed his clipboard to Avery, removed his shirt, and threw it to one side. Assuming an offensive pose, he smiled. "Then let's see what you got, Miss Witch."

The guys all cheered and stepped back to watch the fight. The bodyguard attacked swiftly and dropped her almost instantly. He backed away as she stood. Her amused expression had turned to one of determination. "That's right. Remember why we're out here. It's not all dancing lobsters and jokes."

The other team members glanced at one another as if they'd caught a slight sense of jealousy in his tone, which was ridiculous. The boy had been her closest friend since childhood and there was no way the man could resent that.

Either he felt more strongly about his charge than he would admit to himself, or he was jealous of a lifelong friendship he couldn't hope to equal. Whatever it was, the feeling seeped into his voice and every move he made on the mats.

"You think you're so cute," she snarled. "How cute will you be on your back, looking up at the team after I put you down?"

Lars howled with laughter and pushed her even more. Stephanie watched him closely as he moved in, ready to counteract whatever he tried. His usual closing attack was familiar and one she could rarely avoid. With a swift shift, he would trip his opponent, flip them, and face-plant them in an instant. If it were an enemy, he would follow it up with a knife to the back.

This time, Stephanie was ready for it. She was no longer hesitant when she faced her protectors. As he lunged toward her, she leapt over his sweeping leg and made him stumble forward as he tried to regain his balance.

As he fumbled for his footing, she laughed, pounded her foot into his lower back, and shoved him to the ground. She pivoted and flipped to land on top of him, and her shimmering hand stopped under his chin.

His gaze shifted to hers and she grinned. "What were you saying again?"

From the moment living beings inhabited the universe, there was darkness. Shifty souls planned nefarious deeds deep within the recesses of dark, damp buildings, and all in the name of power and who got to hold it. Once space travel became not only a regular occurrence but something available to those who could afford it, those dark dealings spread across the ever-expanding reaches of space.

Hardened evildoers didn't need to creep around, hoping to not be seen. The enormity of the heavens provided them with ample hiding places. Some chose to float comfortably thousands of miles above their home planet with no chance that their deeds would ever be discovered.

Maintaining their status and not getting caught was the name of the game. Far beyond the outer rings of Earth's galaxy, a group of powerful people sat around a large table and stared at the intel they had received. For good or bad, they had seen the first signs of danger and decided to position themselves to survive it, but they were no friend to the Federation. This made them an enemy to humankind, at least in the eyes of Earth's government.

One man ripped open a nicotine patch and slapped it on his arm. "After all these years, you would think they would find a way to make smoking in space safe by now."

"You would think, after humans are dying off by the millions from smoking, you would have kicked the habit, by now," another said.

The person at the head of the table drummed his fingers against his leg, a serious look in his eyes. The two at the end immediately ceased their banter, cleared their throats, and settled in their seats.

The leader of the meeting shifted his gaze around the table and let it settle briefly on each member before he began to speak. "If all of us fought as one, we still wouldn't win. I, for one, would rather we take our place in power than being ground under their boot. In the first situation, we rule within the new Empire, subjugated, but free. Otherwise, our bones will fuel the fires that destroyed our worlds."

The man beside him leaned back in his chair. "And the blame for it all still lies with the Dreth. They are already up in arms and have pushed forward. Last week, they shot down a Federation Naval ship when they looked like they'd been beaten."

The leader gave a deep chuckle. "Idiots. They did it to themselves."

Another of the men, smaller and older, shook his head before he raised his hand to get their attention. "This coalition has followed in the footsteps of some of the American greats. We will be compared to the British and the French who tried to make peace with the Nazis before World War Two—the ones who knew they'd lose more by fighting than giving in to their demands."

He paused to watch his words sink in before he continued. "They were, in my eyes, the smart ones, exactly like we're the smart ones. We are the ones in power who know the strength of what's coming, and that neither we nor the Federation has any chance against it."

The men all nodded in agreement.

"Yes, of course," one murmured.

"That goes without saying," another muttered.

The older gentleman sighed. "If you had seen what it was like when I was growing up—the way we sat silently while we were overlooked. In spite of how it appeared, the reality was that the power seeped slowly back to us."

He glared around at the others, but none of them said a word. "This time," he continued, "this time, it's better to give in than to be destroyed and left with nothing and nobody, the last of an extinct species. The Federation thinks winning wars is something to be proud of, but survival is the cornerstone to the existence of every living thing in this universe. Survival."

The man at the front agreed vehemently. "And right now, the Federation needs to be coached. They need to be ready to accept the defeat or the treaty presented in order to save humanity—now before billions are killed for some flight of fancy called 'freedom.' There is no such thing as freedom. It is an ideology. Freedom only exists when there is one single master. And in this universe, there are enough masters for each to have a single population."

Another of the men clapped his hands. "When do we begin?"

The leader gave a thin smile that was almost a grimace. "My friend, we have already begun. In fact, others started the movement for us—the degradation of these planets, the loss of lives, the battles within the planet for territory. It started long before us and will continue long after. This is merely a tiny blip in the history of these things. Ultimately, what destroys a civilization are the people within it. We have seen that more times than we can count in foreign, domestic, and interplanetary histories than anything else. The time has come, my friends. We will see a future in the distrust, a future in the tyranny and agony, and it is always the patient ones who gain the prize when everyone else has long vanished, taking each other to the grave."

The guy with the nicotine patch patted it fervently, his excitement rising. "This has been a long and painful trip, but those words make every agonizing, smokeless moment worth it."

The one next to him sneered at him and shrugged, snatched his drink, and raised it. "To more painful moments for our friend here. The more there are, the better we will all be."

The leader smiled as the men talked amongst themselves, a devious glint in his eye.

CHAPTER FOURTEEN

Thumping boots and a creaking floor could be heard clearly in the still, quiet air of a thicket of grossly undercut forest. The wooded area stood deep in the countryside. Old vines twisted through the trees to create interwoven walls almost too thick to hack through.

There, draped over the rickety branches of the trees, they died and left white shriveled nests of foliage. The once lively forest sprawled decrepit and fierce, and secrets traveled through its overgrown paths across the lightly swaying limbs of dead oak trees.

Tucked neatly in the thicket's center, with no real way in or out, was a small wooden cabin that appeared to be abandoned from the outside and like it could simply collapse at any moment. The thumping steps came from within its walls, evidence of a man too lost to step beyond the thicket and back into the real world.

Watching him pace was a second man who held an old quarter-filled bottle of whiskey. He drank and stared at his companion a moment longer before he drifted his gaze to the wall on the other side of the room.

The man who paced, Beta, had led the attack at the Gala. The one watching was known as Crimson. Beta stopped pacing long enough to serve the food from an old wood-burning stove at the back of the hut. When he was done, he returned to the table, balancing the two plates as he yanked out the other old rickety chair.

He sat and shoved one of the plates across to his companion and a spoon a moment later. Crimson looked at the piece of meat, the slice of bread, and the pile of mashed potatoes. When he spoke, his accent was thick and rich with evidence of Russian descent, which denoted a heritage from a place that thrived outside Federation control.

"There has been a day when I looked forward to this type of meal. This is not one of them," he said and poked at the potatoes with his spoon. "We need more to our power suppers than the same two meals."

Beta looked at him. A new scar ran from one side of his face to the other and his left eye remained in its socket but had faded to a very light blue. "We eat what we get our hands on. Right now, we have to wait. I found us this secure location and there will be a drop of supplies and food later this week."

Crimson sighed, picked up the hunk of meat, and bit into it. "Had you told me that by the end of our pursuit of the ambassador, I would live in shithole like this, I would have passed on the job and taken my chances in Russia."

They both raised their spoons to take a mouthful and froze when something tapped on the front door. They looked at each other and Beta's spoon shook slightly. Suddenly, a loud crash outside preceded the sound of their guards grunting in pain followed by the solid thump as they fell heavily.

Odd sliding and shuffling sounds indicated that their bodies were dragged away and finally broke through their shock. Crimson scrambled to his feet, retrieved his shotgun, and checked to make sure it was loaded. The cartridges were in place so he snapped it shut and turned toward the door.

"Knock, knock," a voice called from the other side.

Beta slid his chair back carefully and walked forward with Crimson. Both men came to a halt a few feet from the door. Behind them, shadows danced as a figure lowered herself from the rafters before she dropped the last few feet onto the table. Her boots thudded on the wood and the two men spun and opened fire before they even registered an actual target. Their plates, steaks, and mashed potatoes erupted and smeared down Beta's shirt.

When they ceased their fire, they stared blankly at their mess and the total absence of anybody. The target had left the table as they turned and now crept up behind them and deftly pounded their heads together.

The two men dropped their guns and the intruder snatched them up hurriedly and propped them against the dirty, rusty sink set against the cabin's wall. The occupants stumbled back and clutched onto one another as they tried to regain their balance.

Beta blinked his good eye and growled at their assailant. Their visitor was dressed in a tight spandex suit with a full face mask. From the curves of her hips and firm round breasts, it was obvious that a woman had attacked them. This alone was enough to drive the man nuts since his chauvinism knew no end.

She clicked her tongue, raised the shotgun, and aimed it in his direction. "I know you're trying to hide it."

He glanced at Crimson, who was clearly terrified. "I don't know what the hell you're talking about."

The woman giggled and swung the gun's barrel in small circles. "You know, hiding the fact that you both worked to kill Stephanie Morgana. Trust me, the whole world felt that, and I can promise you that the intrusion on the sanctity of our heroes will not go unanswered."

Beta sneered and his scar pulled on the side of his face. "So, you have come back to avenge yourself, have you, Stephanie? What's wrong? You couldn't get any of your so very brave guards to step up and do the dirty work for you?"

She tilted her head to one side and looked up swiftly as the front door opened and closed. The newcomer had been at the battle too but paid no attention when he walked in. "Hey, guys. I scored some carrots and some kind of mushroom. I'm not sure if we'll get full or get high but what the hell? We're stuck out here anyway."

Laughing, he raised his head and his face paled in shock as he noticed the confrontation. "Who…who is that?"

Beta rolled his eyes. "Stephanie Morgana."

The intruder laughed and shook her head. "Now, that would be nice and poetic, wouldn't it? Except I am not Stephanie Morgana."

His face paled. There was a big difference between revenge and someone sent to kill them. She walked toward the new arrival, raised the shotgun, and aimed it directly at his face. He immediately stilled and she looked curiously at him for a moment before she pulled the trigger. The blast caught him squarely in the center of his forehead. Before his body landed, she sashayed to where the stove stood at the back of the cabin.

She moved the scattered mashed potatoes and meat out of Crimson's seat, turned the chair, and straddled it. After a moment, she used the shotgun to indicate the two men should sit. Crimson obeyed and immediately began to bargain. "I have much money back in Russia. If it is what you're after, you can come with me home I will give you all of it."

The woman put her chin on her hand. "Really? A lot of money, huh?"

He nodded. "Of course. Family fortune is all yours."

She acted like she was really excited, then stood, brought her weapon up, and shot him between the eyes. The impact of the blast shoved him against his chair and rocked him back. When the chair stayed upright, the intruder gave an impatient grunt and marched around the table to kick him in the chest.

The well-placed kick launched Crimson's body and the chair to the floor with a jarring crash. She sauntered back to her seat and focused on Beta. He swallowed hard but returned her stare. He somehow kept his cool fairly well given the circumstances. The only sign that he was afraid was the way he tapped the large gold ring on his forefinger against his belt buckle.

The woman smiled and her mask moved upward as if her mouth curved. "Okay, he bored me. What do you have to say?"

He moved uncomfortably in his chair but said nothing. She sighed and stood to remove a thermal grenade off a loop on her belt. She looked at it as she fiddled with the timing. "Sixty seconds? Ohhhh, wouldn't want to accidentally be too close… let's make this shit ninety seconds."

She strolled across the room and climbed onto a low book-case to place the ordnance on the rafter above. Her lithe jump from her perch ended in a swift kick to topple the bookcase before she aimed the shotgun at Beta. "I wouldn't want anyone to reach it in time."

The man started to stand but she shook her head. "Nah-ah-ah. I want you to know something before you die. That display of villainous treason with the human civilians at the Gala? That was really sloppy. You could have at least blown the ambassador up or something and made something cinematic out of it. But I guess you'll have to wait until your next life, right?"

The man, grimy from weeks of hiding out, sneered and revealed his chipped and yellow teeth. "You'll see this come back on your ass, I guarantee that."

She giggled. "I doubt that, considering you're out here in the middle of nowhere. Anyway, it's been fun. I have to run—you know, what with the grenade and all. I'm sure I'll see you in the streets of hell."

In a single smooth motion, she pivoted swiftly, fired the shotgun, and dropped it as the window shattered. She made a run for it and dove through the ragged aperture bounded by chipped wood and glass shards. Her landing jarred her into an immediate roll across the clearing and into the brush. "Ouch. Oh. Damn. Ouch."

She scrambled to her feet and raced deeper into the forest and as far away from the small cabin as she could. The countdown continued in her head as she flung herself behind a large mound of soil and fallen trees. Pressed against the barrier, she waited impatiently for the blast and was surprised when it didn't come. With a frown, she used her fingers to count another ten seconds and reached zero in her mind before the detonation hurled wood, glass, furniture, and body parts spiraling from where the cabin had stood.

When the last of the debris settled, the woman raised her head, dusted small twigs from her shoulders, and wiped the dust off her mask. Satisfaction flooded through her as she scrutinized the glorious wreck, the building reduced to nothing but a smoldering pile of wood. With a triumphant chuckle, she pulled herself to her feet, stepped through the debris, and looked for any sign that the last man might have survived. All she found was his large gold ring with half a finger still inside it.

She grimaced but laughed almost immediately, shook her head, and clambered over the rubble. A few hundred feet away, she found the backpack she'd left and opened it to retrieve a towel.

After an instinctive glance around, even though she knew she was alone, she tugged the mask off. Her hair was matted with sweat and droplets trickled down her forehead. The afternoon light filtered through the trees and caught Elizabeth's face as she wiped her face and shoved the towel and mask into her bag.

"That damn thing is sweaty. We'll need to mod it. It simply won't do as it is, not unless I want to shrivel up like a prune."

Elizabeth hauled the pack onto her back and tightened the

straps. With her compass, she marked her direction, knowing which way she needed to go to get the hell out of there. She paused for a final look at the rubble, shook her head, and muttered, "Sometimes in life, there is a job that's priceless and you can't outsource it."

She located a stick she'd propped against a tree, drew her machete out of its sheath, and walked through the dark forest. It would be a long hike back to civilization, but no one except the three dead men and their guards would be any the wiser. Everyone underestimated Ms. E, but little did they know she might actually be the best warrior among them—or, at least, out of the ones without magic at their fingertips.

The woods returned to what they had been before her arrival, a graveyard of death. While the trees, shrubs, and animals had innocently died at the hands of man, the three men hiding in their shadows had died for the lives they'd taken, ruined, and changed for the worst.

Their bodies would never see the comfort of a burial plot or be visited by the families they'd left. Instead, their shattered and ashen remains would lie scattered in the barren, unkept forest for the rest of time. Eventually, something would grow there again, but the dust and dirt touched by their bodies would remain poisonous, exactly as they had been throughout their lives on Earth.

Some battles are won to great fanfare, while others are won in the silence of the night when no one is watching, their outcomes never known. This was one of the latter, and no one would ever look for them or grieve their loss. They were the enemy to Ms. E, and her conscience was clear.

Childers put her hand up to Wyld's mouth and shook her head. She pointed at the medals on their chests and a look of comprehension eased across his face. They were both pissed and annoyed at what was happening, but they could only say so much where they were.

He bit the inside of his lip for a moment and came up with an idea. Carefully, he picked his duffel bag up and handed his colleague hers. "Why don't we go for a walk and get some air? We've been dealing with this all day."

She stared at him for a moment but gave him a thumbs-up. "Yeah, sure."

They both headed into different rooms and changed their clothes, folded them neatly, and placed them at the bottom of their bags. With the bags zipped and in hand, they headed out to the lobby. Wyld wore a pair of khaki shorts, a button-up blue shirt, tennis shoes, and a baseball cap. She wore a pair of jeans, a light-gray sweater, and her Federation Navy baseball cap, now battered and worn-in from countless years of training.

"Good thinking," Childers said. "I wasn't sure how to get rid of any bugs that might be on us. I really need to get this shit off my chest."

"Me too," he replied. "Come on."

They headed out of the building and over to his car to throw their bags into the trunk. He started it and they headed away from the base and out of the city to an abandoned warehouse miles away. As soon as the car stopped, they both slid out and checked for any listening devices on the car.

Wyld scanned the vehicle with his detector and shook his head. "We're all clear."

Childers put her hands in the air and yelled in frustration. "What the hell is going on with all this Stephanie Morgana stuff? Seriously. What is it about this case?"

He shook his head, removed his hat, and rubbed his hand through his hair. "I don't know but it's weird. We have higher ups in recruitment asking questions, R&D shoving its nose in, high-up political people who want to know what's going on and 'other players' who are getting pushy about wanting to read reports."

She scoffed and paced rapidly. "Reports we don't have, by the way. Because we can't get an interview request with this bitch."

"Witch," Wyld pointed out.

Childers shook her head and sneered. "Not Morgana. Elizabeth Smith. Which is a fake name or my name isn't—"

He put his hand up. "Don't say it."

She sighed in frustration and her gaze darted around. "Yeah, good point." She scrutinized the area suspiciously but there was no one in sight. "Countries have fallen for smaller stakes than this."

He smirked. "Keep fighting the good fight."

Childers groaned. "You do realize we are caught up in Federation-level crazy, right? That doesn't bother you?"

Wyld shrugged. "Of course it does, but what am I supposed to do? I'm an employee of the Federation."

She leaned against the car. "And this ONE R&D is obviously a front for something. Whoever the owner is, they make themselves as scarce as hell, that's for sure. Not one goddamn trace. It's like the system erased it or something."

"Uh oh. Now don't you go all tin hat on me." He laughed.

The woman rubbed her face. "No. I'm only looking for a way to get past the maybes and what-ifs in this case."

Wyld pursed his lips for a moment before he spoke, not sure he should even put it out there. He took a breath and found his mouth was already talking while his head tried hard to catch up. "We could always try the come-clean approach."

Childers raised an eyebrow. "The what?"

He shook his head. "You didn't listen to tactics in school at all, did you? The come-clean approach. The one where we admit we can't get the legal justification, explain exactly what we hope to achieve and how, and ask for their help."

She stared at him for a moment. "Okay, you know I'm not the

politically astute one here, and I still don't find that a good option at all. I like straight to the point, not straight to the no."

Wyld put his hat back on. "Then we need a plan and we need to work through it fast. This will get away from us quicker than we can piss off a captain, and you know that only takes a split second."

Childers put her hat back on as he moved around the car. She opened her door and looked across at him. "Whatever this is, it's huge. And we need to find it before they find someone to replace us. And I don't mean a new duty station. You know how the Federation handles people who know too much."

CHAPTER FIFTEEN

S tephanie stood in front of the mirror, running a brush through to the silver tips of her long brown hair. She turned her head toward the light and focused on a silver strip near the front, running from hair tip to scalp, her eyebrow raised. It was definitely more noticeable now, but before she could consider what this meant, she caught sight of the news playing behind her.

Reflected in the mirror was a picture of one of the local New Chicago statues of one of the Federation commanders. He stood with his fist out, a famous stance for him proclaiming the land turned toward the future.

However, after some school's-out hijinks, he didn't look the same. The reporter glanced constantly at him as she spoke. "No one claims to have witnessed the crime, but the police believe the culprits are recent Gov-Sub graduates who thought it would be fun to put a hotdog in the statue's hand. They also spray painted his clothes."

She paused while the camera panned to show the graffiti on the statue's uniform, then continued.

"Now, when you drive through this little town, the statue lets you know this Federation commander not only likes his hotdogs but that he is—and I quote—'down with the Gov-Sub Seven.' Exactly what that means is yet to be revealed."

Stephanie giggled as they showed pictures of the statue, the stone spray-painted to look like the general wore a t-shirt and baggy shorts. The hotdog flipped continuously as the reporter spoke, then the station returned to the news desk.

She was about to go back to examining the silver streak in her hair when the word "Dreth" scrolled across the screen and caught her attention. Slowly, she turned, the brush forgotten in her hand as she watched.

The reporter looked concerned and close to tears. "There has been a clash between Dreth and Federation ships in Deep Space Quadrant 768 early this morning. Using the new speed-of-light data transfer, the Federation Navy picked up the report shortly after it occurred and have declared themselves victorious despite sustaining heavy losses and severe damage."

The anchor turned away from a screen depicting the aftermath of the battle as the camera switched angles to show the faces of two obviously important men.

"In other news, two powerful business moguls, Don Kefferman and Stephen Brightfield were gunned down today in what is being termed a business-on-business mogul vendetta. Apparently, the week before, Kefferman and Associates lost a valuable bid to corporate rivals, Stephen Brightfield and his agency."

After a dramatic pause, the anchor continued. "Kefferman had started out on top but from what he told business associates, the Brightfield agency made illegal bids and used bribery to devalue his offer. Both men were pronounced dead at the scene."

The anchor turned toward the front and a smile brightened her face. "In more entertaining and exciting news, TRQW will make a global broadcast featuring the Federation's first witch. This special feature will go live in four weeks' time."

Her co-anchor took a sip from his coffee cup before he cut in.

"Oh. yeah, I'm all about watching that. The girl is definitely a hero, not to mention super-hot."

Stephanie curled her lip in disgust, turned to the mirror, and brushed her hair a little harder than normal. She hadn't given anyone an interview, let alone agreed to being the subject of a special feature. There was no way to understand how TRQW—or anyone else—could do full-on specials about her without ever having touched base.

How would they really know anything about her or her life? A knock on the door interrupted her indignation, and she set the brush down. She strode to the door and flung it open to reveal Elizabeth, who stood with her hand half-raised to knock again.

For a moment, she froze in surprise, then stepped aside and forced a smile. "Come in."

The woman accepted her invitation and Stephanie turned away, using two fingers and a downward swipe to mute the television.

Ms. E watched the girl walk back to the mirror, pick the brush up, and run it through her hair. Stephanie's eyes took on a blank look and she knew the answer before she asked the question. "Did you see all that on the news?"

She nodded. "I did. It's so dumb."

Her visitor walked over and sat on the edge of her dresser. Crossing her legs, she looked at the girl. "Stephanie, I want to talk to you about something."

Stephanie glanced at her. "I already had that talk, and it was a long time ago, trust me."

Elizabeth snorted and shook her head. "God, no. Not *that* talk. I'm your boss and your friend, not your mama. And I would hope you've had that talk. You're a grown woman, after all. Anyway, what I wanted to tell you is that you need to decide if you'll pay attention to the news about you, or live your life how you want to and ignore it."

She stopped brushing for a second, her mind racing. "Uh...okay."

Ms. E released a deep breath, picked a bottle of perfume up, and focused on it rather than her companion. "The reason you need to do this is simple but important. Once you start down the road where you focus on what others say about you, it's too late to change what the future holds."

She looked to see if the girl was listening before she continued. "Your subconscious will always think about what the talking heads might say, and it'll become second nature to adjust everything you do to make yourself look good in their eyes. It's called being human."

Stephanie scrunched her face in confusion. "So...ignore them?"

Elizabeth shrugged. "That's completely up to you. It's for you to decide what is best for your future. No one can decide that but you."

The girl put the brush down and ran her fingers through her hair. "I guess you're right. Listening to the news report negative things about me will only bother me. They'll only cause me more anxiety and bring me down. Although it would be nice to watch the good clips."

Her mentor shook her head. "Those can be as devious as the bad. Then, you're teaching your brain to only seek out the good stuff and that it needs to find ways for you to do more of it." She shrugged expressively. "Sometimes, it feels like you need the emotional equivalent of ice cream to get through an existing crisis. Personally, I'd suggest you have a really good AI filter through the feeds to find what's right for those moments."

Ms. E slid off the dresser and walked to the door. She placed her hand on the doorknob, then glanced over her shoulder at her friend and ward. "But then, that's only a guess."

She winked and walked out, shutting the door behind her.

A little while later, Stephanie stood in the training ring, sparring with Avery. The rest of the team was using the weights and working out. Lars did laps around the perimeter and watched the sparring so he could step in to assist with the practice if they needed it.

Today, they did more team-on-team work, even though it never seemed to be enough. Avery knocked her feet out from under her and she flipped forward to land hard on her stomach with a grunt. She used her magic to propel herself upright and tossed her gloves angrily to the floor.

Lars jogged over to them and stood in front of her, his stare a little concerned. "What's wrong with you today?"

"This, right here—it's not real life," she snapped and spread her arms wide. "All it's doing is getting me in better shape. And don't get me wrong, that's great, but this isn't like a real fight. This is exactly what the Virtual World was made for. To get us working as a team inside a simulation instead of practicing out here with no way to know what will happen when we reach any particular moment in a battle."

He nodded and put his hands on his hips. "Right now, this is the best option we have. There are a million tactics, even inside the Virtual World, that you can practice and still be useless as a team. I—"

Stephanie raised her chin and she grinned as she pivoted away from him. "Hold up. I'll be right back. I gotta talk to Elizabeth."

Avery glanced wide-eyed at Lars. "Oh, this isn't good."

She hurried out of the training room and down the hall to stop in front of Elizabeth's office. After a moment, she cleared her throat and knocked hard, then stood and waited. The woman opened the door, a sandwich in her mouth and folders in her arms. She waved her inside and set the files down before she put the sandwich on a plate beside an already opened can of Coke.

"Hey," she said once her mouth was clear. "What's up?"

Stephanie walked over and sat down on the edge of a chair. "I wondered if there was a way we could all do a Pod exercise. We would need enough equipment for maybe twenty people."

Ms. E looked surprised. "How would we get that in here?"

Stephanie bit the inside of her cheek, a little startled as she hadn't anticipated a less than excited response. "There is still the advanced pod at TimeWarp. We could rent the place while the pods are on order."

Her mentor choked on a sip of Coke, astonished that she thought such a thing was feasible. "Do you have any idea what that would cost?"

She shrugged. "All I can do is ask. If it isn't possible, maybe we can have the team go to a local place here in town and meet me in the Virtual World. TimeWarp has to have a franchise that's not too far away, right?"

Elizabeth sat and rubbed her temples. She could already tell the whole thing would be one giant headache. "So, what exactly do you want to accomplish and how?"

Stephanie scooted back and rested her arms on the chair, feeling the same surge of energy she'd felt the first time she'd ever negotiated with Elizabeth. "I want to train my people to help train me in tactics in locations we don't have access to. Being all together as a team can only help us. We don't have that feeling when we're training here in the gym. After all, it's exactly the kind of thing the Virtual World was built for."

The woman pursed her lips and stared at her desk while she thought about it. "I'll run it past the boss, but don't get your hopes up. I think it makes perfect sense, but it's a huge security risk."

"Thanks." She smiled and stood. "And try to breathe. You look like you'll have an aneurysm any second."

Elizabeth gave a short bark of laughter and waved her out of the office. When the girl had shut the door behind her, she picked the phone up, muttering to herself. "I look like an old hag who never sleeps. Oh, wait, that's probably because I *am*."

BURT picked up the call and noted it still crackled with a strange static before the call went through. "I am in the middle of something. I should be done in three minutes and twenty-two seconds or so."

She shook her head at the odd phrasing and leaned back in her chair while she waited. Another factor that added to Burt's mystery was the fact that he was so specific with time. He was either a savant, on the spectrum...or... Well, something else—and that was simply too much for her to even contemplate.

Exactly three minutes and twenty-two seconds later, Burt came back on the line.

"What can I do for you?" he asked.

Elizabeth took a deep breath. "Stephanie came and asked if we could work out how she could get twenty people into pods for a group training session. She really wants to work in the Virtual World with her team."

When Burt didn't interrupt, she went on. "She had a couple of ideas, like all of them going to the TimeWarp in her home Sub or one of its closer franchises, or the team going while she stayed here and they met up inside the Virtual World. We can't do it here, though, because we literally don't have enough room to set up more pods at this location. We'll blow the whole system."

"Hmm," Burt said, sounding strangely robotic. "I guess we didn't think of all contingencies our pupil might need. She raises a good point, and it is something I've thought about anyway. I want a place like the universities have, and this gives me a good reason to build one and use it for Stephanie."

She took a bite of her sandwich, glad it wasn't a video conference. "It'd be easier to simply buy out a failing university. Find one that was trying to do the right thing and—"

"What did you say?" Burt asked.

"Buy out a failing university," she repeated. "An existing university would have what you want. It would have the right building, an off-grid power supply, all the pods, teachers who'll need employment and be grateful for it—everything. Simply because it's failing doesn't mean it wasn't any good or didn't have adequate facilities. Some or most of the failures are because they attempt to provide a more equal education system and no one wants to fund them. They can't keep up with the expense of what they're trying to do, and those who do have the cash don't want them to."

Ms. E took another bite of her sandwich, chewed, swallowed, and sipped her drink while she waited for Burt to answer. When she was done, there was still silence on the other end of the line. Raising both brows and tilting her head slightly to the side, she cleared her throat. "Are you still there?"

Burt came back on the line. "I am. I apologize for the delay. I was testing your theory and you are right, there are seventeen universities which meet your criteria. Based on news reports and other data, three of them might fit the model for being more altruistic than capitalistic. You will need to do other tests to find out which of them would best meet our preferences."

Elizabeth was still stuck on "news reports." She opened her mouth to ask why her boss thought they were a reliable source of information but changed her mind. To be honest, she really didn't want to know the answer.

He continued, oblivious to her confusion as he talked about the potentials he'd found. "However, there is only one that has enough pods at this point in time, and it would probably appreciate the income it would receive from renting out both them and a week's worth of accommodation."

Elizabeth shook her head. "A week?"

"Yes," Burt replied and sounded as if he thought it made obvious sense. "I need at least a week's data of Stephanie being in space before she goes to Meligorn so that she can test her theories on gMU. Once she is on the ship, her opportunities to undertake Realtime research will be substantially reduced."

"That's one way to say a reduction in communications will send us back to prehistoric times," Elizabeth snorted.

"It's only hours," he replied.

Elizabeth nodded. "Yes, I stand by what I said. Prehistoric levels."

BURT had already run prehistory of the colonies through his system. "You do know that they didn't even have smoke signals in prehistoric times?"

"How would we know?" she asked. "We lost most of our history books and others have been proven to have been changed to support the winners."

He gave a fake human laugh. "It is highly unlikely that the winners of pre-history are cooking the books to make themselves look good."

She shrugged. "It could happen. Humans are devious."

"I've noticed," he responded, making Elizabeth think he might actually have cracked a joke. But no, he merely wasn't done. "I saw that the surviving individuals responsible for the Meligornian attack have sadly died from lead poisoning."

"Pity that." She gave a disapproving sniff. "Nice change of topic."

"I try," he replied. "Is there any chance of finding out how exactly they died?"

"Not unless the dead can come back and change history." Elizabeth smirked.

"I see," he responded. "Well, I would hope that if there was somebody—anybody—else involved, they were careful not to leave even a flake of skin at the scene."

Elizabeth yawned. "I'm sure they were. Professionals are simply that. Professionals."

"Oh, here we go," Burt replied in his oddly never-changing

tone. "I found a school not too far away that we can rent and which is willing to sub-divide its system so ONE R&D can have sole access to the data cable and ensure nothing routes through their core servers."

"Yeah," she said and wrote the information down. "Like I'd trust them to fix their firewalls appropriately."

He paused for a moment. "Have I explained to you how much I like you?"

She smirked. "No, but a bonus goes a long way toward letting me know I'm appreciated. Just saying. The key to my heart is not to turn me into a goddess because I already am one. It's putting the credits in my account."

"I'll keep that in mind," Burt replied. "I have transferred the base information to your terminal, so we can discuss this further later. I have some system repairs to work on. If you need anything, you know how to contact me."

"Mhmm," Elizabeth replied.

She hung up and looked down as her tablet chimed to let her know her bank account had been updated. Flipping to the appropriate screen, she smiled. There'd been a new deposit. "Now, that tells me you really, *really* like me."

Chuckling, she logged out of her account, slid the small tablet into her pocket, and grabbed her mobile. She had to get the team packing. With as much as it would cost to rent a university, they didn't want to miss a second of the time they'd paid for. They had to be packed and ready to roll, ASAP.

As she reached over to turn off the desk lamp, she smiled. "Good thing I don't do this for money or I wouldn't need to work again for a decade."

She walked out of her office, turned, and stared at where the symbol for ONE R&D floated on her screen. "Thanks, boss. I like you too."

CHAPTER SIXTEEN

Stephanie, Elizabeth, Lars, Avery, Johnny, Frog, Brenden, and
Marcus stepped out of their flying SUVs, their bags over
their shoulders or across their backs. They all stared at the
campus of Harbor Technology U in amazement. It was very
appealing and so different from the compound, with broad,
grassy lawns surrounding three tall buildings set close together.

It was nothing like Pinnacle. At that university, they'd manu-
factured virtual grass projected onto their grounds and other
high-end pretensions. This college actually had the real thing. In
the pods or out of them, they would be in a beautiful place.

A woman in a pencil skirt, matching suit jacket, and a white
blouse walked across the grass to greet them. She must have paid
attention to the pictures Ms. E had sent because she smiled as she
stopped in front of her.

"You must be Elizabeth."

Ms. E turned her attention to her and noticed the single
strand of pearls at the woman's throat. "Yes. I am. You must be
Mrs. Braddock, head of the Administrative Division."

"That would be me," the woman confirmed with a little side-
step as if she were dancing.

She pointed to the building on the right. "On the bottom floor, you will find a large bank of pods. We don't have our students stay in them twenty-four hours a day like some universities do, so your dorms are above them. The registrar has your room keys and allocations. I'm sure you can allocate them as you see fit. Let her know which names to assign each room in the database. The university's IT specialist is scheduled to come by to check out the lines at—"

She stopped as Elizabeth shook her head. "No. I don't want our pods to access your data, and I certainly don't want my data on your side. That way, the Feds won't have any access to our company's proprietary information, and they won't be able to accuse you of having a commercial interest so they can tax you to death."

The woman's face took on a look of concern and she touched the tip of her chin with her perfectly manicured fingers. "Oh. I hadn't thought of that at all. In fact, none of my administrative or technology specialists have thought of that either. I would have assumed that such a liability for the university would have been common knowledge."

Ms. E smiled and put her hand on the woman's shoulder. "It is, but not everyone pays attention to that class in their Freshman year. Don't worry, though. Trust me on this. I have both our organizations' best interests in mind and I want this to go as smoothly as possible."

Mrs. Braddock nodded vigorously in agreement, and Elizabeth continued. "I certainly don't want any hiccups like having a Federation Navy or the Federation Governance Board coming in to take advantage of our information."

She allowed a dramatic pause. "I need to know that the separation between the university's information and our company's is so secure even the Federation hacking teams can't break through it. That process will also make the university's data more secure, as well."

Lars leaned over and spoke softly in Avery's ear. "I'll kick your ass so bad you'll be bowing to the Master of War."

Avery snickered. "More like the Master of Disaster."

Elizabeth had left Mrs. Braddock and headed toward them. When she arrived, she clapped vigorously. "All right, kids, let's go upstairs, decide your room assignments, and find your pods. I have a couple of things to take care of. Give the pods a general run-through to familiarize yourselves, but don't start until I give you the word. This will not be fun if we wake up to find the whole of the Federation has studied us while we were in there."

She pursed her lips and watched as the team hurried off, acting like children. Shaking her head, she followed Mrs. Braddock into the main building and took the elevator down to the server stations.

When they arrived, her guide looked at her. "Everything you will need will be right here. If you have any questions, let me know."

"Thank you," Elizabeth replied, faked a big smile, and ignored the faint uncertainty on the woman's face.

As soon as Mrs. Braddock had disappeared from sight, Ms. E dropped the smile, pulled her bag around, removed her laptop, and connected it directly to the system. The elevator opened again, and she paused as a guy in a Harbor Technology shirt walked over. "You Elizabeth?"

She looked down at herself. "Last time I checked."

"I'm Joe, your consultant," he said and shook her hand.

"Nice to meet you, Joe." She clicked the button on her laptop to run the tests she needed to do. "I have taken the liberty of looking for any security slip-ups before you get in there. It should save you time."

The computer dinged and they both leaned over to read what it had found. There were eleven more problems apart from the ones she'd found already. "Okay, so I need you to review and fix these and I need it done so fast you forget there used to be dial-up."

Joe shivered. "That was the worst period of time in history. Sure, when it first came out it was slow, but we knew nothing else. When the wars were in full swing and all we could do was use dial-up service, I started to hate technology."

Elizabeth gave him a half-smile and tried not to be too rude. Hopefully, he'd get the hint that she wasn't there to debate technology, shoot the shit, or become bosom buddies. She needed the system online and secure or they would waste the valuable resources already invested in bringing them all the way out there.

As she stood, she unplugged her computer and gave him space to work. "Here's the deal. I need you to make damned sure this system isn't screwed with. No one enters or exits without my express permission, which you most likely will never receive because I can't think of a soul I would share this with. I pay really well—which you already know from the fee I've paid to get you out here today. But the termination clause, if you screw me over, is a bitch. It's not a bitch for me, it's a bitch for you. And we aren't talking a little fine or penalty."

Joe caught the meaning in her eyes and swallowed hard before he nodded vigorously. "Right. It's okay. I've got this. No one gets access to this system. Period. Or I will find myself in a dark room with no windows and doors if I screw it up."

She smiled brightly. "Good. I like you."

The team stood around the pods, holding the specialized cleaning equipment as they gawked at the setup. Most of the guys hadn't actually been inside a pod since high school or college. A few had used them briefly to gain specialized training, but after that, all they'd had was fieldwork.

Pods were like a party to them. They got to train without the painful aftermath. That and Frog was hell-bent on choosing a specialty outfit for his time in the Virtual World.

Stephanie was glad to see them so happy, but the pods were nothing new to her. She was used to being in them, even if one differed from another. Avery finished wiping the screens down inside the last one and stepped out of it before he dusted the top off. "These are really nice. Not Morgana quality but definitely nicer than anything I've been in before."

Brenden and Marcus pushed buttons and watched the bed compression go up and down. "Yeah, I thought this university was more altruistic. We heard they were one of those asking for Federation bailouts but because they didn't move with the status quo, they might not be able to stay open. I figured there would be like shitty beds in here."

She stood and rubbed the dust from her nose. "This place is very new in the grand scheme of the universities. It was an altruistic effort but not funded well enough by 'hard' businesspeople who marry altruism to finances. Unfortunately, they didn't realize that because of the way the Federation is set up."

"Greedy and money hungry?" Marcus asked sarcastically.

Stephanie smiled as she continued. "They didn't put enough stock in the businesspeople willing to invest. They didn't realize that right now, with the way things are, corporate backing is essential. Investors are literally what makes the system work like it's supposed to. They tried to do it all through public money. It didn't work because those who had the money took it to the higher, older, and better-ranked universities."

"So, what is ONE R&D doing renting here? Why didn't we rent from one of the others?" Avery asked.

"Two reasons," Lars replied. "One, security. This school understands our need for privacy and anonymity. They were willing to do whatever it took to secure our data and keep our data-stream separate from theirs."

She nodded. "Yep. And number two is that the amount of

money ONE R&D is paying will get them through the summer and part-way into the fall semester. It basically buys them time to find out exactly what they need to do in order to stay open."

Brenden ran his hand over the outside of his pod. "Hopefully, they don't sell out, but I guess with the system working against you, it's not hard to see why some do."

Elizabeth came down the steps into the server room and tapped her watch. "All right, buddy. Are we good to go or should I clear you a dungeon seat?"

The consultant stood and closed his laptop. "We're all good to go. Rock solid, airtight, and worm proof. No one will get through that bitch."

She raised an eyebrow and retrieved her tablet and cord. "Let's double-check that, shall we?" she said as she plugged it in, ran a simulation, and scrutinized every line as it moved through the system. When it was done and her security suite gave it a green light, she smiled. "Good work. You get another day of smog-infused sunlight."

Satisfied, she sent Stephanie a text, giving her approval for the team to start the training sequence. When she ended the call, she sat on the stool in the server room and exhaled a deep breath. "Now, we wait and see what happens."

CHAPTER SEVENTEEN

With the pods clean, the team had returned to stow their gear in their rooms. As soon as Stephanie received the go-ahead, they dressed in their pod gear and headed down again, ready to rock and roll. They didn't know how long they would be in, and they didn't care.

Technically, the machines were able to sustain their occupants for up to two weeks. The school only used them on a day to day basis, with one small four-day stint for intensive training immediately prior to exams. The guys didn't care about that. They slid in quickly, leaving Stephanie and Lars on the outside to make sure the initial immersions went well before they joined them.

He gave her a crooked smile and she grinned in response as she dipped down, lay inside the pod, and pulled the lid closed over her.

The lights on the ceiling lit up at intervals and the cleaning solution's floral and fruity smell surrounded her. She had to admit, she enjoyed being able to get in and out of her pod without being naked. That aside, from the controls and the wear on the cushion beneath her, she definitely missed the quality of the one made specifically for her. She hated even thinking it because it made her feel like the red-headed kid who had been behind her in the Gov testing line. Still, she couldn't help it because her own pod was so damned comfortable.

The AI walked everyone through the procedure, took their vitals, hooked them up, and sent them into the Virtual World. As each Avatar appeared in the common room, they looked around and studied the small separate platforms on which each one stood.

It looked like a Federal military installation, but the older parts and gross smell screamed Dreth. When Frog appeared, he looked at his jumpsuit and shook his fists in the air. "Nooo. I had plans."

Lars appeared beside him and smacked him on the back. "Sorry, buddy. You'll have to play dress-up some other time. I'm sure we could set up a play date for you and Avery's niece."

Avery snorted, drew his gun, and examined it. "I wouldn't leave him alone with my niece."

Frog rolled his eyes. "Yeah, yeah. I never get a break."

Everyone looked up as Burt's voice echoed from above them. "Hello, team. For those of you whom I have not yet had the pleasure of working with or speaking to, I am Burt, owner and financier of ONE R&D. I wanted to take a moment to say hello before I hand you over to the administrator."

Everyone responded with a greeting, although not very enthusiastically. BURT remained but altered his voice to that of an AI. "Greetings. I am Joan, your administrator and AI for this training session. This specific simulation was pulled from the Federal Navy operations vault. It was taken from a small operation that went bad for the Navy when they faced the Dreth on-world. The Navy uses this operation—or modified versions of it —to see if the gamers can come up with better tactics than their own men."

"Why do I feel like that would be a yes?" Avery chuckled.

The AI paused. "Actually, you would be surprised. The simulation has a 96.9% fail rate for first-time users. The other 3.1% is made up of first-timers to the simulation, who have previous experience in virtual games like it. This is a very challenging scenario, but only a taste of what you will face once you have passed the simpler versions."

Marcus frowned. "Did she say, 'a taste of?' Since when did AI's use slang?"

The comment made BURT realize he was far more advanced in language than the typical AI. He hastily forestalled any other questions. "It is now normal for all AI's to be updated with advanced language capabilities. We are not only shown the formal language but slang and historical terms, as well. This allows us to understand our user on a better and more accurate level."

Stephanie rolled her shoulders. "So, Joan, what is the first scenario?"

The room spun around them and slid to a stop as the platforms on which they stood became a single floor. The world rotated, and they emerged in a frozen tableau between the Federation military and alien forces. In the center, more affluent individuals were negotiating for better assistance programs for the Dreth.

The AI explained. "This is one of the more horrific situations the Navy faced with the Dreth. They gathered for one of their usual political meetings where they discussed the reconstruction of Dreth and the issues the world might face under the Federation."

Studying the scene, Stephanie found it hard to believe, but the AI continued. "This meeting was what sparked the fires of revolution on Dreth. It was the point where discussion ended and violence spread beyond the pirate world itself."

A short silence followed as though the AI gave them time to consider the importance of the scenario before it continued. "One important thing to keep in mind is that the Federation's representatives had to be familiar with Dreth physiology and movement in order to realize that their representatives had been substantially offended. Had they known that, they would also have known that the only appropriate and permissible course of action for Dreth leadership was, at that point, a martial response."

Avery raised an eyebrow. "Why does that sound like it was a very bad thing?"

The AI continued. "If you miss the appropriate physical cues, you will be unable to discern the Dreth preparing to do battle directly in front of you. That is a surprise that no human wishes to encounter—and one which no one survived in the original scenario. Now, prepare your weapons and remember, you are soldiers and guardians of the Federation, so act accordingly."

The AI faded when BURT muted his presence so they would assume he wasn't there. As the simulated presence vanished, the scene came to life and the team focused on the humans, who talked between themselves before they turned to the Dreth.

The man at the table folded his hands in front of him and stared at the alien lord as if things were a joke. "We understand that you want to keep your world as you see fit. But if you want our help, you'll have to let us advise you of any changes you need to make to how things are done here. We may find better ways— more efficient ways—to help. Hell, we may even learn better ways to handle things on Earth from you."

The man leaned back and spoke to his Federation companion from the side of his mouth. "Like how to walk around in a shit-hole and not contemplate the genocide of an entire race."

He might have thought his words hadn't carried, but Marcus thrust his arm out and pointed at the Dreth lord and other high-ranking aliens behind him. "There it is—the sign Joan talked about. Their scales rippled with a reddish hue. Most wouldn't notice it, but that color indicates a deep and pure level of offense."

Stephanie nodded. "All right, team, ready yourselves. They're preparing. We want to be able to act at their first move, but not too early. In a real-life scenario, we wouldn't expect this. We would have had to be a whole lot more observant."

She began to pull magical energy into herself, determined not to allow what had happened to Frog happen to one of her guys. Her mind focused, she flexed her hands and prepared to shield her team from harm above everything else.

The scene remained calm for a moment longer before the first Dreth made his move. As soon as he did so, her team yelled as one and unleashed holy hell on the alien leadership.

The Dreth protection team was shocked and slightly thrown off by the surprise defense. It was something they obviously hadn't seen coming. Stephanie raised her hand, now shimmering with light, and ran it over her face.

Her features remained the same but she was now covered in a constant shimmering veil. The mask wavered over her to blur her features like a holographic overlay gone wrong.

She couldn't see it, but when someone else looked at her, they wouldn't be able to tell who she was or that she was using magic. The effect was designed to help keep her abilities secret until the situation reached the crucial moment when she needed to use them.

It didn't take the Dreth team long to overcome its initial surprise, and they responded with a concerted attack. Stephanie's team fought back and dealt with them either by killing or stunning them, or both.

During the battle, she used several subtle spells to hinder the enemy, but nothing they would notice and trace back to her. When all the aliens were dead, the simulation paused, and a woman walked out from the back of the treaty room

She was tall and dressed in a black skirt suit and six-inch heels, with a black lace veil over her face to keep her identity hidden.

"I am your over-viewer," she announced. "You may call me Strike. At the end of each battle, I will deliver an After-Action Report analyzing your actions. Listen to my comments. They could mean the difference between life and death in the field."

Frog leaned toward Marcus and whispered. "Is she an AI? Because whoever created her did a top-notch job. Look at those legs."

Marcus smirked. "It's all fun and games until you lift that veil and find your Great Uncle Herbert."

Inside the school, after the students had all gone back to their dorms for the evening, the chancellor called a meeting. He sat with two important financiers and one vital analyst at the table, sipping coffee and scrutinizing the numbers.

The topic was one of those none of them wanted to deal with. The outcome usually worsened every time they met to study the finances. This time, though, it proved a welcome respite from the usual doom and gloom.

He closed the file, removed his glasses, and looked at the team. They responded with relieved smiles, all glad to have found the small glimmer of hope that had been painfully absent in their business connection to the university for quite some time.

"I want to thank whoever put that report together. We needed those insights on how to use Federal money so we could come close to breaking even next semester. The money from ONE R&D has given us the time we need to try to save the school."

The chancellor looked at the team, but not one of them took credit for it.

"There's no name on this report, sir," one of them said as he flipped through it. "In fact, there are no identifying marks at all."

Oblivious to the meeting closing in the other building, Stephanie's team were busy controlling a small squadron of armored flying modules. These were tall, tank-like ships sent out from cruisers during space battles for "man-to-man" combat, so to speak. Their presence meant less carnage on the battlefield since both sides tended to hold fire from the bigger ships while the modules battled it out. They were, in essence, the combat troops with the ships serving as fortresses.

She flew forward, directly in the center of the squad, while the men flew close behind her and to each side. "All right, boys, let's try to keep ourselves out of the firing line. Light their asses up, and if you can, knock the comms out and the weapon ranges on the main ships."

They called their battle cries as she led them in, firing as she went. Her team swerved skillfully across the sky in evasive maneuvers while they delivered a sustained attack against their opponents.

Frog and Marcus spotted the comms tower first. It was hidden behind a large front-facing wall at the top of the ship. "We got this, boss. You keep the firepower low there in the middle."

Stephanie looked around warily, a strange sense of caution nagging at her. Frog and Marcus whistled and yelled as they careened through the enemy fire and up to the wall. She zig-zagged until she made it through the hatch into the docking bay of the Dreth ship. The others followed and touched down behind her before they leapt from their modules to race toward the internal doors.

She linked to Frog and Marcus and confirmed that they were headed for their target. "Boys, you need to be careful. There's always extra protection at the towers."

Frog scoffed. "Puhlease, these giant idiots don't have the brains to think up something that simple."

As they accelerated in a direct approach toward the wall, a flash of light caught her attention. She altered her scan to reveal a grid-like wall of lasers guarding the tower. Her face paled as she screamed over the comms. "Abort, abort! Marcus, Frog, there is a laser field beside the tower. I repeat, a laser field. *Abort!*"

Her warning came too late. They were going too fast and neither of them noticed the other defenses the Dreth had laid until they were a few feet away from the grid. Before their modules struck the lasers, hatches opened on either side of them and Dreth warriors stepped out onto the hull.

They were anchored to the ship with metal belts and held enormous guns. Before Stephanie had time to warn them, the aliens had unleashed an intersecting field of fire on the two armored modules to destroy their engines. The craft spiraled end over end into the waiting grid.

With a cry of pain and outrage, she pulled on the gMU she could sense all around her. Her eyes turned black and she gritted her teeth against the pulsing galactic energy.

As she watched Frog's plane shatter into space debris, she used the screen inside her helmet to target the battlefield. Her breathing grew faster and shallower as though she was running a race, and then, she stilled.

In her helmet, she located her targets and used the module's sensors to show her magic where to go. Between one quick breath and the next, she thrust a huge ray of energy from her hands and screamed her grief to the stars.

The beam rocketed out of the docking bay, guided by what she could see in the helmet. It obliterated the Dreth ambushers who were too slow to retreat into the ship. It leapt from the deck to the comms tower Frog and Marcus had been so intent on targeting. And, after that, it demolished the enemy's fighter pods and tank modules and the cruisers' guns and navigation systems. Still rampant, it plunged into the ship to destroy the Dreth themselves. Any enemy not incinerated by the beam itself were sucked into space.

The team gathered and guarded her back while they watched

her with sadness in their eyes. They knew she was angry, but her anger manifested in a way that could kill not only the enemy but herself as well. The scene paused and Stephanie released the magic. Her eyes slowly returned to normal.

Strike walked into the stillness to critique their training. She stepped through the vacuum of space and onto the deck of the Dreth docking bay and began going through the list of mistakes everyone had made. This included Frog and Marcus who appeared in the team's ranks.

Then, she turned to Stephanie and put her pen down. "And you. That was completely irresponsible, childish, and reckless. You lost your damned mind. You no longer led your team but put them at risk."

The girl lowered her head as the AI faded and they were returned to the common room they'd started in. The team gathered around her to give her comfort and pointers.

Marcus squeezed her shoulder. "I think it would have helped if you'd commanded us to stop and told us to haul our dumbasses back to where you could kick them."

Frog nodded sagely. "Yeah. You know what they say about splitting the party."

Before she could reply, Lars interjected. "You do know that when you go all nutso crazy magic lady, you block us out, right? People die in war, and if you don't get used to that without completely hulking out, you'll end up costing yourself and the rest of us our lives. We're your team, your family. Connect with us so we can work as a single unit, not a group of individuals seeing who can be first to get our dumb asses killed."

By the time they'd talked to her, the day's training was over. Part of Stephanie felt bad, but the other still felt the burn of watching her men die. She couldn't allow that to happen in real life. Not ever. And never again in the Virtual World, either.

CHAPTER EIGHTEEN

The next morning signaled the start of a new day of training and Stephanie was in the mood to beat the system. She was tired of failure and of letting her magic take control. Still, it wasn't something she really knew how to handle.

She would simply have to make sure her team stayed safe while they accomplished the mission. They started the day with a team breakfast and then headed for the pods. Lars got a kick out of how tough Marcus and Frog acted whenever they walked past the college girls who clearly wondered who they were.

When they reached the pods, Frog wouldn't shut up about it. "Yeah, they were like, hey, what's up?"

Lars laughed. "Yeah, wondering why the senior center was visiting."

Marcus joked. "Frog, the old man."

Frog snarled. "Get off, Marcus. You were as bad. I saw you puff your sparrow-sized chest out."

The other man made a muscle. "Sparrow chest? More like a rhino, bitch."

Stephanie slapped the top of her pod. "Everyone, shut it. Get in game mode and go in. We have to focus. If we don't, when we reach the real scenario, we'll all die. Do you want to see that happen?"

The guys quieted instantly and shook their heads as they went to their pods. She tried to ease up a little. "Good. Let's meet inside."

Elizabeth walked away from the main pod room as the team climbed in. She headed down the hall and to the left to quietly enter a side room reserved for lecturers. With the door securely closed behind her, she smiled and opened the pod located inside and sat on the edge to remove her shoes.

That particular room was not only set aside for lecturers, but it was special, as well. Located in the same data stream as the team's pods, it allowed BURT to hack in and speak to her as an AI.

He, of course, changed his voice from the one he used on the phone. However, since the only ability he had to "hear" was to compare the tones of a voice, he didn't realize that the one he chose was similar enough to his phone voice to make her suspicious.

The suspicion was nothing new, of course. It only added to the boat-load she'd already collected and stored in her head. This was no time to consider it, though. "I need a special setup, AI."

"What would you like?" BURT answered.

She thought about it for a moment. "I want the operation to start in a bar on a Space Station. This is how it will go…"

"I assume this is some kind of relax mode until the setup is ready." Lars shrugged and looked around the bar with the rest of the team.

Frog sniffed and smiled at the odor of stale beer in the air. "I miss that smell. Lockdown has been hell. Can you get drunk as an Avatar?"

Marcus rolled his eyes. "No. You can taste it, but it has no physical effect on you."

The team found a big table to the side and gathered around it. Marcus and Frog raced for the chair and Marcus got there first, knocking the other man to the floor. "Ha! Loser. I guess you get to buy the first round."

The other man stood and grumbled. "Assholes. One of these days, I'll be the one who saves the day and then everyone will want a piece of me."

"Gross," Brenden teased. "You'd let us take a piece of that? Sorry, bro, but I'm into chicks. It's cool if you're not."

Frog tried to respond but instead, waved his hands in a gesture of frustrated surrender and headed to the bar. He stepped into an empty place at the counter and caught the bartender's attention. "Six beers, please. Your house draft."

The bartender poured the beers and gave him a tray to carry them. Smart avatar, considering he was notorious for sticking his fingers in a person's beer to get it where it needed to go. He put the tray on the uplifted palm of one hand and held the edge with the fingertips of the other. Turning, he bumped lightly into a guy. "Sorry, dude."

The guy turned, and Frog registered two Dreth standing behind a human in overalls. The aliens both had beers in their hands and snarls on their faces.

They stepped forward and said something in their language. The human turned, laughing, and gave one of the warriors a high five. "Good one, dude."

"I'm sorry," Frog said, irritated by the whole situation. "What did he say?"

The guy turned back, a smirk on his lips. "He asked when they started letting the poor kids into the party."

He gritted his teeth but took a deep breath, nodded curtly, and maneuvered to walk past them. As he turned, he muttered under his breath, "Dreth-loving bitch."

The stranger must have heard him, because he grabbed his arm and spun him back, the smirk gone. Frog managed to keep the beers on the tray. "What the hell did you say to me?"

He shook his head. "Nothing worth repeating."

"You think you're hot shit? Is that it?" the guy said and, without waiting for a reply, he raised his hands and shoved him in the chest.

Frog watched it happen as if he were caught in slow motion. The tray took flight, beer spilled everywhere, and the glasses plummeted to the floor and shattered.

Without thinking, he snapped his hand up and caught the heckler by the wrist. "That was a bad move."

Back at the table, the team discussed one of the fights from the day before. They had won it, but it had taken them curling Frog into a ball to send him through a tiny duct and out the other side to successfully complete the mission.

They all laughed wildly as they relived the moment but Stephanie jerked her head around. Immediately, her eyes turned black.

Everyone rose as one and Lars reached for her as they looked for their teammate.

The guy broke Frog's grip and thrust him back. The bodyguard glared at his opponent before he looked down at his front and swiped at the beer that had settled on his ship suit. "You douche. There's beer all over the place. I should make you clean it up. But it's your lucky day and I'll give you a pass, so back the hell off and go your own way."

The Dreth and the human exchanged glances and laughed. "Or what, little man?"

Before Frog could answer, the lights over the bar and in the ceiling began to flicker. The beer in the man's hand shimmied and shook before the glass exploded. One by one, every glass in the bar began to shatter to strew the floor with shards and brews. Frog, the asshole, and the two closest Dreth looked around and tried to identify what the hell was going on.

Frog had a fair idea. He glanced at the table, where Stephanie stood facing them, her eyes black and a wild wind blowing her hair around her head. He could almost feel the rage dripping from her. "Oh, shit…"

She stormed forward and pushed him out of the way to grasp the guy by the throat. He gurgled in protest when she picked him up and hurled him over the bar. Her gaze immediately sought the two Dreth warriors. She was coming unglued and as soon as her fist pounded into the first alien, she began to attack in full force.

That was when the rest of the bar joined the fray. Dreth, Meligornian, and humans alike entered the melee. Magic erupted everywhere, and she beat the hell out of the two Dreth who had messed with Frog.

The woman in the veil walked out from the kitchen behind the bar. Her shoes crunched on the glass scattered over the floor. "*Stop!*" she commanded, and the entire scenario froze. This time, even Stephanie and the team were trapped in place.

For an AI, Strike was extremely attractive. Today, similar to the days before, she wore a sleek black dress but instead of a veil, had added an all-black mask to cover her face. No one could see her lips move when she spoke, but they could all hear her. She pointed at Frog. "Wrong. You should have immediately gone to the team. No words. Your pride almost got you killed."

Her arm shifted to the men at the table. "Wrong, wrong, wrong, and wrong. Not only did you let Stephanie beast-out like a maniac, you didn't even try to stop her. No one watched her closely enough, and none of you watched Frog's back in an unfamiliar bar in an unfamiliar part of town. Did you forget this was a training exercise? Not a single one of you paid attention to shit."

She whirled and walked over to Stephanie, tilting her head so that she was eye to eye with her. The girl lowered her gaze, the only thing she could move at that point. "And you? Right now, you're the team disaster, not its leader. You didn't lock down your emotions and this space station is simply one giant spaceship. If you wreck the walls in here, you'll *all* tread vacuum. Dumb-asses."

After a moment of stunned silence in the wake of her tirade, she looked up. "AI, put Burt on the line. How did Stephanie connect to her security guy inside the Virtual World? She could feel him in trouble. I saw her pivot to find him before he even got hurt. Do you allow that?"

BURT paused, a little startled by the question, and tried to compute the implications. "No," he said finally when he realized she was waiting for a response. "They've never been in trouble together before."

There was a moment's pause and they both realized what had happened. The woman looked from Frog to Stephanie. "She's connecting in the real world while she's in the Pod. Then, she is reacting *inside* the Pod. So, while Frog's avatar doesn't have any emotions, she felt Frog's emotions while he was across the real room in his pod and she found the problem inside."

"Your analysis appears correct. This will be a challenge," Burt admitted. "I wonder if there is a distance attribute."

The woman groaned. "Can you stop extrapolating data for five seconds?"

"Data is life," he replied, still clearly distracted.

The woman threw up her hands, exasperated. "Whatever. That might be the AAR, but I want the rest of you, as a team, to figure out what you need to do to help Stephanie control this or it will be the end of all of you."

Having delivered the After-Action Report, she released them by keeping the bar frozen but allowing them to move. Stephanie rubbed her fists. Lars and Marcus talked for a moment to the side and then Lars stepped forward. "Maybe we can try something that will pull you out of your own head. Something that can click with you so you can try to pull back when your emotions threaten to take control."

She nodded. "Like what?"

Marcus smiled. "Like a code word. Something you care about."

The other man sighed and gritted his teeth. "Marcus felt 'Todd' would do it."

Stephanie looked at them and raised her eyebrows. "That should do it for sure. But who knows? Anything is worth trying, at this point."

The team resumed their place as the AAR Avatar began the scene from where they left off. Stephanie could see the damage she had done. The Dreth and their human were in really bad shape. The team worked with her to complete that run and get them all to safety. It wasn't ideal, but it worked to keep them intact. Once they'd reached sanctuary, they restarted the scene.

This time, the entire team remained watchful, waiting for something to go down. As soon as Stephanie felt the anger in Frog, her head whipped around and she simultaneously pushed from her seat. The bodyguards sprang into action and raced around in front of her to block her view of the fight. Lars grabbed her cheeks and looked into her ebony eyes. "Todd. Remember, Todd."

She shook her head and blinked the black from her eyes before she looked at them, nodded, and patted Lars on the shoulder. The rest of the simulation was nothing more than a good, old-fashioned bar fight. In fact, it was quite funny to watch. She stood to one side and shielded her magic from those in the room so they wouldn't recognize who or what she was.

With a small gesture here and one there, she slid small balls of magic into the melee. One knocked bottles onto a Dreth's head. Another sliced through the waist on the human's overalls so the bottom half dropped around his ankles. A third tripped one of the aliens so he fell face-first into the lap of a very large and sweaty man.

Once Frog's fight was taken care of, she smiled and entered the melee to work off a little of her anger. She threw punches with real enthusiasm and laughed as Lars pounded a Dreth in the stomach until the warrior fell. Catching his eye, she nodded at her strong arms. "It's like a workout, but faster."

"Hell yeah." He laughed. "That's the kind of fight I want. Get in shape."

"Break some noses," she added as they high-fived.

Stephanie sat on the edge of her dorm room bed and stretched her arms and legs. She hadn't told anyone, but while they woke from the training feeling perfectly fine, she felt every punch, kick, and muscle strain from inside the Virtual World. Her muscles were getting stronger and her body thinner, and usually, every step she took hurt like every day was leg day in her workout routine.

She looked at her watch and smiled as she hauled the phone beside her and dialed her parents' number. A holographic image appeared of her mom and dad sticking their heads close together as they waited for their archaic communicator to bring her up. She knew when it happened because her mom's face went from puzzled to excited in three seconds flat.

"Hi, guys." Stephanie giggled.

"My baby," her mom greeted her excitedly. "I've waited all week for this."

"Hey, sweetie," her dad called and waved enthusiastically as he backed up and sat on the couch. "How's work going for you?"

"Good." She smiled and eased her sleeve down surreptitiously to hide the bruises on her arm. "How's it going for you? Is the cleaning doing well?"

Cindy rolled her eyes but in a relieved way. "It is going really well. There are a couple of people working for us now who we hired on as security. I really didn't want to feel that way about a job but several of our cleaners were getting harassed—"

"And your mom," her dad interjected.

Immediately, Stephanie frowned. "What?"

"It was no big deal." Her mom shook her head. "They took care of it, and that includes your father who punched one of them in the mouth. Now, he has swollen knuckles."

He held his hand up with a proud grin. "All in a day's work."

She laughed. "Good for you, Dad. You are the beast. Seriously, the beast."

Her mom sighed. "I didn't want to get anyone hurt but you know how protective this family is. I can only imagine what it would have been like if Uncle Jimmy and Uncle Eddie had been there. Those poor smart-mouths wouldn't have walked for years. But anyway, no need to rehash. What did you want to talk to us about?"

Stephanie smiled and bounced slightly on the bed. "I have to go to Meligorn for the medal presentation, so I've decided I'll come home before the trip. I want to see you guys and Todd, and I thought why not visit my favorite people in all this world before I visit some strangers in a whole other system."

Her mother leaned her head against her father's shoulder. "You are the best daughter ever. This will be a fantastic visit."

CHAPTER NINETEEN

The team opened their avatar eyes and stared at row upon row of weaponry. The AI spoke before they could make any comment. "Welcome to another day of training. Today, you will be placed in a situation created specifically to meet your training needs. Please take two minutes to prepare for battle. You may take anything you can carry, as long as it doesn't impede the other players."

Stephanie didn't move because the only thing she needed was her magic. The other guys frowned and studied the array of weapons. Lars walked along the line of guns, not knowing where to start. There were Dreth weapons and Federation weapons, and everything was fully charged. Even Meligornian batteries were available but none of them were ready to try their hand at magic. That was her thing.

Frog rubbed his hands together and selected a couple of daggers, two grenades, and a bow and arrow off the shelf. Marcus gave him an odd look. "Okay, Rambo Robin Hood, what the hell will you do with a bow and arrow when you face a Dreth?"

He stowed his gear and ignored the jibe. "Hey, I could totally kill a Dreth with an arrow. I simply have to hit that one spot under their chin that isn't tough."

The other man blinked at him. "Really? This coming from the guy who almost axed himself in the foot because he didn't let go of the ax handle when he tried to throw one at the Renaissance Festival when we were kids?"

Frog groaned. "You always gotta bring that up, don't you? We were kids, damn it. I got this now."

Marcus shrugged and walked over to the pistols. He selected two but changed his mind and only took one. "Suit yourself, but don't throw that thing anywhere near me."

Brenden chuckled and slid a half-sword in a back sheath. "Who the hell thought we'd need gear? We always appear with weapons and we're darn good in hand-to-hand combat."

The AI spoke. "Please line up on the white line. The simulation is about to begin."

The room went dark for a few seconds before the lights returned. The team stood inside a bunk room on board a ship. Everything was painted gray and with a small window. Marcus stared out and angled himself so he could see one of the tail fins behind them. "Hey, this is a space liner. We must be downstairs in the crew's quarters."

Before any of them could respond to that, a sudden shudder distracted them and they exchanged glances before they opened the door to their cabin and hurried through.

With the corridor clear, they raced along it until they found the steps leading up. They took these two at a time, readied their limited selection of weapons, and looked for the source of whatever trouble had caused the tremor.

Stephanie shook the magic down into her hands and followed the others around a corner. They all froze as the Dreth pirates boarded the ship and immediately hurtled down the corridor toward them.

Surprised and outnumbered, they failed the scenario. In less than fifteen minutes, they were dead—although, oddly enough, Frog was the last to succumb. When they opened their eyes, they were back in the armory room.

"You have two minutes to prepare," the AI told them.

This time, the team rushed through the weapon racks to select what they needed. Even Stephanie armed herself, knowing that magic wasn't the only tactic she had—and that it wasn't always the best tactic, either. That was especially true for a prolonged battle where she didn't want to wear herself out by using too much magical energy.

When the scene changed to signal that the scenario had started, they wasted no time. They raced out of the room and up the stairs, loading their weapons on the way. This time, they were the first to reach the main deck where passengers boarded—the same one the Dreth would use to board the liner. Lars and Brenden went to work to rig booby traps for when the enemy broke through.

Once that was done, they withdrew into the corridor and waited, their guns ready. The hatchway burned white and erupted inwards. Huge Dreth pirates followed seconds later, bellowing at the top of their lungs. The team looked at Lars, who held the detonator for the traps. He pushed it and they all winced and covered their ears as the grenades exploded in sequence to obliterate several of the pirates.

More followed, and then even more, until Stephanie thought there was a never-ending supply. She was also grateful that they'd chosen a single entry-point, which meant that she and the team didn't have to split up to deal with them all. In this scenario, they could hold the entry until their guns ran dry...and then they could use the guns of their enemies.

When the flood of aliens slowed to a trickle and finally, to a drop, they were left facing one last adversary. He was smaller than the others, climbed cautiously over their corpses, and immediately dropped his weapons when he saw the team. With his hands raised in the air, he waited for them to stand and face him in the corridor.

When no other aliens followed him, Stephanie slid a magical mask over her face and stepped into view, Lars beside her. "Stop right where you are."

The Dreth laughed and gave her the finger as he began to speak. "On this ship is a very, very large bomb, only waiting for the connections to touch." He giggled and twitched and his hands fluttered nervously above his head. His eyes glowed as though he wasn't entirely sane.

She put her hands on her hips. "Oh yeah? Prove to me you can set it off."

The Dreth slowly opened one of the hands he held above his head. Nestled in his palm was a small black box with a button in the middle, and his thumb was set squarely against it. "I let go, you go boom."

Stephanie pursed her lips. "So, I guess you can't let go."

He grinned and whispered, "Boooom."

She smiled and threw her arm up quickly and a shield hurtled toward him. It wrapped around his hand, forced his fingers closed, and kept his thumb pushed firmly down on the switch. It was exactly what she had tried to accomplish, except that it also severed his hand at the wrist "Whoops."

The Dreth shrieked and fell back. Dark-green blood fountained from the wound to pool on the floor around him. Frog grabbed his stomach and gagged. Lars shook his head and turned to her.

She closed her eyes, then opened them again and stared intently at their faces as she spoke. "Okay, there's a bomb on this ship. We need to find it, and most importantly, we need to get it off the damn vessel. There are a ton of civilians here who have no idea. Marcus, Frog, you go with me. Lars, Brenden, Johnny, you take the lower levels. If you find it, call it in and move with it."

The team nodded and hurried away, heading to search their

designated section of the liner. Lars sent a couple of images of what they should look for to their headsets, but it didn't really help. After searching each section as thoroughly as they could, they all met on the main deck once again, each one breathing heavily. Lars shook his head. "Nothing. We found nothing."

Stephanie nodded. "Yeah, we didn't either."

Frog leaned his hand against a grey box on the wall. "Where the hell is this thing? I'll be pissed if its right in front of our noses."

The whole team turned toward him and froze. He frowned. "What? Why are you staring at me?"

Lars put his hand out. "Hey, Frog? Buddy? I think you should take your hand off that metal box with a blinking red light on the front of it. And maybe do it real slow."

He swallowed, but he kept his eyes on Lars' face. "What box?"

Lars tried for a nonchalant shrug but didn't quite manage it. His voice cracked when he replied. "You know, the one randomly stuck on the wall behind you."

Frog looked along his arm to where his hand rested on the box. Instead of slowly, however, he yanked his hand off like he'd been burned. He offered the team a shaky grin. "Uh…found the bomb."

They'd all been so busy watching him and the bomb that none of them had noticed Marcus leave. He returned, almost tripped over one of the fallen Dreth, and cursed softly as he guided a one-man luggage drone through the air beside him.

"What?" he asked when he saw the looks on their faces. "I saw one of these in a thriller I watched once. Some spies doing stuff on an interstellar cruise. I thought there had to be some truth in the background and found the drones were real and stored behind the concierge's desk around the corner."

He eyed the bomb and guided the luggage drone to where Lars stood. "That should fit, right?"

"Nice thinking," Lars told him and nudged the drone carefully into place.

Marcus fiddled with the controls and it hovered alongside the box. He touched the controls again, and a panel slid open in the top to reveal enough space inside to fit a small suitcase. "Do your magic, boss...or get Brenden to do it for you. Either way works for me as long as you don't set it off."

Lars rolled his eyes and took a closer look at the bomb.

"It looks like one of them slapped it on the wall as they came through." He glanced through the boarding gates and smiled. "They left their umbilical intact when they boarded. I wonder how much time we have before they decide it's time to leave."

Stephanie watched as he turned his attention to the device on the wall.

"I hope this thing is as simple to remove as I think it is," he muttered, retrieved a couple of tools from his belt, and worked them deftly around the edges of the device.

Brenden came over to help him, and between the two of them, they lifted the bomb off the wall and set it gently inside the drone. Once it was nestled and secure, Marcus used the controls to close the top and then looked at Lars.

"I'd say we should send it back to them, but they're still attached. How about we seal this deck, instead? That way, nothing can sneak in while we put this sucker out through one of the docking bays."

Having taken a tour of the lower levels, Lars knew exactly where to go. He led the way while Marcus followed, steering the luggage drone through the corridors. Fully loaded, a row of green lights now glowed steadily around it to show it was in use.

Lars took them to a small docking bay where the liner's shuttles were stored. The team scrambled hastily into emergency suits, attached tethers, and opened an airlock leading to a maintenance hatch beside the docking bay doors. Once the airlock had cycled closed behind them, they watched as Marcus steered the drone out of the liner and as far as it would go.

Stephanie walked up beside them, her hand wrapped around the Dreth hand with its scaly thumb pressed against a button on a small, square box.

"What?" she asked and held her grisly handful tighter. "I have to hold the damn thing in case the magic wears off. He almost blew us up with this."

Marcus frowned and looked out into space. "See that blinking light?"

He pointed to where the luggage drone was little more than a glittering speck, its green lights flashing as if it knew it was no longer on board and tried to tell the universe of its distress.

She nodded. "The bomb is all the way out there. Let's light this sucker up."

He kept his hands on the drone's controller to avoid a risk that it might fly back to the ship under some emergency protocol, but Lars nodded. "Do it."

Stephanie held the controller up and tried to pull the dead pirate's thumb off the switch. The Dreth's hand had stiffened and wouldn't release it. She rolled her eyes and grabbed the thumb and fingers in an effort to pry them apart.

At first, they didn't budge and she renewed her efforts. Finally, with a sickening crack, they loosened and the controller fell. As soon as the pressure was off the button, the bomb detonated to create a momentary flare of light that faded quickly to nothing. Well, almost nothing.

Marcus pointed out into space. "What is that?"

Stephanie and the others gasped. It was a piece of the drone, it's lights still gleaming, and it was on a direct trajectory toward them. For a minute, it made no sense and then they realized there would be some kind of shock wave from the explosion.

Lars slammed his hand on the controls for the maintenance hatch, trying to force it to close faster. None of them could leave the airlock until the outer hatch had closed, and the green-lit fragment of debris streaked ever closer.

They heaved a collective sigh of relief when the hatch *thunked* closed and the inner hatch started to cycle. It opened in the same moment that the blast struck the liner, rocked it sideways, and sent them to their knees as they flung themselves into the ship. Instantly, the emergency protocols came into play and hatches snapped shut, compartmentalizing the ship to maintain its atmosphere in case the hull was breached.

Stephanie clicked her tongue. "Well, I guess he wasn't bluffing."

The team staggered to their feet and Lars looked around to make sure they were all okay. "Now what?"

She looked at the Dreth ship still docked to the Federal liner. "I guess we have to board the Dreth ship."

"If it's still attached," Frog muttered gloomily.

Marcus clapped him on the shoulder. "There's only one way to find out."

They all agreed and stripped out of their emergency suits to head back to the main boarding area. Lars spoke to someone on his comms halfway there.

"What?" Stephanie asked.

"I told the captain to keep everyone in their cabins," he said. "We don't want any passengers or crew walking about until we can get this mess cleaned up."

They raced back to the breach point, using the emergency override codes Lars was given by the captain to open and reseal each bulkhead they encountered. To their relief, they discovered the Dreth had used a hard dock rather than an umbilical to gain entry to the vessel.

Instead of blowing the passenger entry, they'd pierced the liner's outer hull and used clamps to drag the two ships closer before they temporarily sealed the two ships together. The mystery of it was why they hadn't released the clamps, dissolved the seal, and left. The team crossed into the other ship and ran through surprisingly empty corridors to find only the occasional Dreth body and rooms stockpiled with food.

They'd explored most of the ship when Stephanie entered another hallway and her magic woke and jolted a charge of energy through her. She followed it, found a large metal door, and called for Johnny, who removed the covering from the control panel and managed to activate it. As soon as the entrance was open, they both moaned and covered their noses and mouths.

For the first time, she questioned the wisdom of not staying in the emergency suits. They would have slowed the team down and none of them were used to wearing them, but they'd been stupid lucky not to have needed them.

The smell that surged over them was unlike anything she'd ever experienced. She put one foot inside and stopped to stare in shock and disbelief. Bodies lay everywhere, both human and Meligornian— children, animals, and the beaten and bruised corpses of over a dozen different women.

Johnny put his hand on her shoulder and pulled her back. He wrapped his arms around her and turned to pass her to Lars. "You shouldn't have had to see that. I'm sorry."

Before she could react, the scene faded, and she stood wrapped in Lars' arms with her team surrounding her in a large, beautiful Meligornian field. Strike appeared and stood before them, but it was Elizabeth's voice that echoed from the speakers. "Very good, team. I'm sorry you encountered bodies. I'm sorry that the universe is such an ugly place."

Stephanie folded her arms. "I don't know why that was necessary. All those women and children. It was horrible."

Ms. E hadn't liked including that part of the scenario, but it had to be done. "Stephanie, my job here is to prepare you for anything you might face out there. Like I said, the universe can be a very ugly place, and you have to grow up sometime. Better you do that in here with people who care about you than out there where people will try to use or hurt you in some way."

Stephanie remained silent and simply nodded her head in understanding. The AAR AI began her report, went through the different sections of the fight, and broke them down into things done well and things done badly. This was one of the best scenario completions they'd managed. When the report was over, they woke in their pods.

Elizabeth stood beside Stephanie's and put her hand on the girl's shoulder as she climbed out. "Everyone, go clean up, but before you head to bed, meet me in the common room. I have an announcement."

She turned her head to her charge. "Are you all right?"

She nodded and rubbed her forehead. "I know there is even worse than that out there. I know that in my life, I will probably see things that will never leave my mind. I guess it's not a bad thing, though, to be sad about it when you see it. It shows I still have some empathy and caring left in my soul."

Her mentor hugged her. "You have so much caring and empathy, I doubt you will ever lose it. You have to protect your heart, and you have to protect your soul. Everything else will be okay if you can keep those two things safe."

Stephanie pulled back and gave her a tight-lipped smile before she headed off to take a shower. The woman shut the pod and sighed. This was one part of the job that no one wanted to deal with.

Once they'd showered and changed, the team made their way back to the common room. Everyone wore their pajamas and looked dead tired. Stephanie walked carefully and tried not to reveal the amount of pain she felt from the last session. When they were all seated, Elizabeth looked around. "Where's Frog?"

"I'm here," he yelled as he slid around the corner in an adult-sized Superman onesie.

They all chuckled as he took his seat and grinned from ear to ear. Elizabeth shook her head and laughed softly, the first real laugh she'd had in days. "All right, family. We have our travel information for the trip to Meligorn."

Everyone but Stephanie cheered. It was hard to cheer when she could still see the bodies whenever she closed her eyes. The older woman watched her as everyone settled again. She felt for the girl but knew there was nothing she could do to fix it.

This was something else she would have to work out on her own. That was simply the way that it was for every warrior, soldier, and mercenary in the universe. For Stephanie, though, Elizabeth knew such carnage would never become commonplace or easy to deal with.

With an effort, Ms. E shifted her attention to the group. "So, the good news is that the Meligornian king and queen will pay for everyone to go to Meligorn, and not only those receiving awards. They know we're a team, and even if you weren't at the Gala, you were part of the reason those fighting fought so well. So, make sure your toenails are clipped, and you lose the... What did you tell that man at the party? Wash the idiot out of your mouth?"

Everyone laughed and Stephanie managed a smile for the first time since she'd left the pod. She nodded and shrugged. "Hey, sometimes, you have to tell them how it is. You can't let these idiots keep walking around here like that."

"That's the truth," Frog replied and shot the others an evil look.

"Awe, Frog is butt-hurt," Marcus said and laughed.

"I think I would be too if someone put toothpaste in my shampoo and shampoo in my toothpaste," Johnny quipped and laughed hysterically.

Elizabeth gave Frog a pouty-lipped glare and continued.

"Make sure you clean up well because you will represent ONE R&D and the first witch of the Federation in front of Meligornian royalty…and may God help us all."

The guys all put their hands up in the air and cheered. Lars grabbed Stephanie's hand and raised it, and the gesture made her laugh. In turn, that made her relax and her team filled the hole she'd felt had been carved in her chest ever since she'd climbed out of the pod. She stood and raised her hand to silence the group. "And one more thing. We will make a pit stop at my house to see my parents. So, please, try not to embarrass me."

"We'll be as good as angels," Johnny said, painting a halo around his head with his hand, and blinked as innocently as he was able.

Frog ran up behind him and stuck two fingers on either side of his forehead like horns. "Demons posing as angels maybe."

That night, they all went to bed in a good mood—laughing, singing, and ready to head out into the universe after an intense week of training. Not every day had been good, but not every day had been bad either. They had clicked at some point and really started to look and feel like a team. That was something none of them had dreamt would happen that fast.

The next morning seemed to come too soon for Stephanie, who heard the alarm and dragged her sore, tired, and bruised body into a seated position on the edge of the bed. She grunted with pain as she lifted her leg and pushed her fingers down her sore calves in an attempt to loosen them. Everyone was packed and ready to head back to the home base, and all they had to do was have breakfast.

She took her time getting dressed, not really hungry in spite of the workout she'd had. It didn't bother her, though. She was merely happy she'd slept through the night without any nightmares from what she had seen. The whole scenario had begun to feel more like a dream or a movie scene than reality. It still wasn't something she could wrap her mind around, but now, she didn't have to. She decided that was probably for the best.

On the trip home, she curled up in a corner of the car and pulled her phone out. She had a missed call from Todd, and simply seeing his name made her feel better. Once she listened to the voicemail, she'd call him, knowing he had no idea she was coming to visit. Not unless he'd already run into her parents.

"Hey there, Stephie," he'd said in his message. "I was hoping to get ahold of you. I guess you're off doing some crazy saving the world shit, though. Tell Batman and Superman I said hi."

Stephanie chuckled as he paused for a moment. "I...uh, I ship out tomorrow to boot camp. We start on the ground and then head up for space training. I keep remembering how you said to be careful and I wanted you to know I was listening."

His voice caught a little before he continued. "Besides, I can't go and die on you, you know? Who would you turn to for your pop culture knowledge? It would be lost for all time, and that's too sad for our story. It would never make it to production. Anyway, you are the bestest best friend a kid could have. I will write you if they let me have paper and a pen, and you better be there at boot graduation to see me all fly in my uniform. I'll put T. Cruise to shame. Love ya."

The message ended and she sighed, realizing he had left the message the day before. She was shocked that he'd shipped off so fast and had thought he'd at least wait until the end of summer. Then again, he was champing at the bit to get away from his family, and school was over. There was nothing really to keep him around. She hoped that when she got home, things would settle, even if it did feel weird without him.

Once she'd arrived and everything had calmed after the initial excitement of reuniting with her parents, Stephanie snuck off to her old bedroom and pulled some of her nicest clothes from the closet. She remembered when she first ordered them.

Holding that memory close, she put on the blue wrap dress and pulled her hair into a low side bun. After she'd applied makeup for the third time because she kept screwing it up, she stared at the girl in the mirror and barely recognized herself. She had been stuck in ponytail-save-the-world mode. There really wasn't time in there for blush, eyeliner, and mascara.

Seated at her desk, she cleared a space and set her phone in the middle of it before she opened her portfolio. The number she chose was one of the two sales calls she'd promised to make. The lead had come from her mom, who'd met the man on an elevator ride to the top floor of Mr. Martelle's building. Stephanie dialed the number and put it on speaker, smiling as soon as his face appeared and floated above her handset.

"Mr. Harper," she said, her smile warm. "This is Stephanie Morgana representing—"

"The cleaning company," he finished happily and cut her off. "Yes, I spoke to your mother not too long ago. Yesterday, in fact. To be honest, I almost canceled this meeting."

"Oh no," she exclaimed and looked shocked.

"I know." He chuckled. "But I came in today to discover the cleaning company I hired have shut their doors. No notice, no nothing. Just done. Gone. So, I guess you're my angel in disguise."

Stephanie gave him an appreciative laugh and launched into the details of what her parents' company could offer. Mr. Harper listened attentively and asked a couple of questions here and there, but nothing she hadn't expected. By the end of her spiel, she couldn't tell if he was more interested in her or the company, but either way, she had his attention.

"What do you think?" she asked him. "The sales projections, the increase in your business, and the influx in hiring that goes along with it will require you to have a crew you can rely on. I think that if you accept a bid from my company, you will never go to anyone else."

He sat there for a moment and his expression revealed that he was deep in thought. Then, he nodded. "I agree. You've bothered to get to know my company, our sales goals, and what our business entails. That makes me trust you and the company you represent. Have your mother and father write up a contract. I'll look it over, and we'll go from there."

Stephanie gave him a thankful smile. "Thank you, and we'll talk soon."

"Oh, and Stephanie," he replied. "Congratulations on the Meligornian award. You definitely deserve it."

She couldn't help but grin as he hung up and his hologram disappeared. As the last of it faded, there was a knock on her door and Lars stuck his head in. "Whatcha doing?"

"Running big business." She turned and crossed her legs daintily.

Lars whistled as he noticed her dress. "Look at you, all dolled up. How'd it go?"

"He wants a contract from mum and dad asap," she told him proudly.

Marcus stuck his head over Lars' shoulder and Frog poked his head under his arm. "That's what I'm talking about. Let's go celebrate, girl."

Stephanie thought about it for a moment and shrugged. "Why not? Give me five minutes to pull on some jeans, though. This outfit is strictly for when I need to impress."

The team flew into the local bar like wild people who hadn't had any free time in what felt like forever. They talked, laughed, told stories, and even managed to get out of there without any crazy fights like they'd had in the training session. Of course, in that bar, there were no Dreth hanging out and everyone cheered them like heroes. The guys loved it, and it took an act of God—

or, in fact, the bar closing—to get them out of there and over to the hotel.

Stephanie's parents had come along and laughed as they listened to the team talk about their lives before Stephanie, their upcoming trip to Meligorn, and how she was completely superbad when it came to fighting. Her father gave her a fist-bump while her mother pouted, not wanting to think about her daughter in any fights.

As they turned the corner leading to the hotel, still laughing, they found themselves face to face with several members of the local gang. Their laughter died abruptly as they eyed the men cautiously. She recognized them right away, having watched them gather every night at the Gov-Sub park since she was a little girl. They, however, didn't recognize her. They only recognized what they thought was a good chance to get their hands on some cold hard credits.

"Well, lookie, lookie, lookie." The leader laughed. "All these guys and the one stepping forward is the tiny little girl."

Stephanie smirked and cracked her knuckles. Behind her, Johnny grabbed her parents and yanked them back to make sure they stood where he could protect them. Lars, Brenden, Marcus, and Frog stepped forward, two on either side of her.

The thug shook his head. "This is even better. Four flyboys and a little girl gonna take on the Hoods… What are you—Stacy from the block?"

She managed to keep a straight face and raised her hand to silence him. "Keep it to knives and lower and we won't have problems. If you draw a gun, your life is forfeit."

The gang members shrugged but seemed to agree, and the two sides stared at each other for a moment longer before anyone moved. When they did, it was all together.

Stephanie hurtled forward, dropped with one leg bent and the other straight out, and slid across the sidewalk. She ducked low as she closed with the first gang member and pounded her fist directly into his nuts as she skidded beneath him. He groaned and made a gurgling noise as he clutched his crotch and fell forward.

Lars winced and grasped her hand to help her come up out of the crouch. He didn't let go and she glanced at him, trying to read his thoughts before she followed the direction of his gaze. His gaze shifted to watch the two guys creeping up on them, and she smirked. She took hold of his other hand and prepared for what came next.

As expected, Lars waited for the right moment and heaved upward to swing her around in a circle and raise her legs off the ground. Her heeled boots slammed into one, two, and then three of their opponents. The attack either knocked them out or dazed them to the point of uselessness.

"Let go when you hit four," she yelled.

Lars did exactly that and flung her with the full momentum of the swing. She twisted and drove her legs into another of the hoodlums. He tumbled and she landed above him with one foot on either side of his face.

Both sides managed a few good blows, but not a single one of the gang members were able to touch her. She was far better than any of the Hoods, there was no question about it. From his position as bodyguard, Johnny leaned in to watch and laugh at every good strike she made. "Oh, I taught her that move—it took her a few times to get it right—oh, damn. Nice punch."

He glanced at her parents and noticed they were reacting quite differently to the fight. Her dad seemed enthusiastic, shifting from side to side, and had his own small silent celebration every time she kicked someone's ass. Her mother, however, had gone into shock and stood there with a confused look as she watched her baby girl act like not such a baby anymore...or maybe a baby monster.

"Actually," Johnny pointed out in an effort to distract her. "Frog taught her the kick to the nuts. He has no shame—"

Stephanie vaulted upward and landed to see only three Hoods ranged against her. The one in the middle looked at his defeated comrades and shook his head. "This is bullshit."

He reached for the gun shoved into the front of his pants. When he pulled it clear and looked up, a bright blue translucent shield protected the team and her parents.

She, on the other hand, was on one knee, her head low and her arms out to the side. When she raised her head, her eyes were dark. "I told you, no guns."

The gang members scrabbled at one another in an effort to find safety in numbers. "Oh, shit, it's that Morgana bitch."

Two of them bolted, their legs moving as fast as their feet could make them. The third shook his head, aimed his pistol at her, and prepared to fire.

She raised her hand and magical energy blew wildly around it. As she moved to block his attack, a shot rang out and the ganger fell and clutched his arm. She turned. Johnny stood behind her, lowering his gun with a serious face.

Stephanie released the shield and stepped forward, her eyes still black and an angry wind started to swirl around her. Lars hurried forward and grabbed her hand to hold it tightly. "Don't do it, Stephanie. The paperwork for killing him is a pain in the ass, trust me."

For a moment, she stared at him, then looked back at the gang member who sat on the ground and moaned in shock. She stepped forward and came to a halt beside him. He stopped groaning and looked fearfully at her. Leaning over, she gave him a good look at her wild, black eyes. "It's Stephanie from the Block to you, bitch."

Having delivered that line, she swung her leg back and kicked him repeatedly until he fell unconscious. Sirens blared in the background and the team started to move. Lars grabbed her and smiled, nodding toward the not-so-distant sound. "Let's get out of here."

CHAPTER TWENTY

"Remove your civilian clothes, put everything in the box labeled with your family's address, and get dressed. Now is the time to do any last-minute checks, go say goodbye and kissy-kiss your mommies, and break up with your girlfriends." The boot camp instructor walked around, his face angry, his arms bulging, and his uniform perfectly creased.

Todd sighed and removed everything from his pockets, then dropped his phone in the box. He saw a notification on the device and leaned over hastily to grab it before the instructor could close the lid. The man glared at him as he clicked on it, took one look, and laughed.

Stephanie and her team appeared on the screen, beating the living hell out of a group of gang members from his Gov-Sub home. A reporter came on and the video continued to play next to her.

"It's only at the end," she said, "that you can see her power. When they drew a gun, she didn't hold back. But even then— even in the heat of the moment—they only shot him in the arm to incapacitate him."

The video stopped and didn't show Stephanie kicking the ganger into unconsciousness, which was probably a good thing. The camera zoomed in on the reporter. "It seems the witch Morgana isn't as scary as some would have us believe."

Todd snorted and leaned his head back. "You have no idea. You had better never truly piss her off."

As rapidly as he could, he opened an email and typed his message. As he pressed send, the instructor blew a loud horn right beside his head. "Drop the tech in the box, momma's boy. It's time to get back to your roots. Now, get dressed double-time. Move it! Move it! Move it!"

Todd dropped the phone in the box but noted the sent symbol as it landed on top of his clothes. He grabbed the Navy issue sweatpants and shirt and dragged them on. As he pulled on his white socks and service-issue tennis shoes, he wrinkled his nose.

The instructor stopped next to him and the recruit straightened to stand tall. He glanced at the box, all sealed and ready, and down at the sweat suit. "What's wrong, recruit? You don't like your smurfs?"

"They are perfect, Petty Officer," he yelled in response.

The officer sneered and flipped his hand through the young man's hair. "You will be up front and number one when we visit the barber. Shears out, bitches. You are losing your lovely locks. Time to become a soldier in the Federation Navy! It's time to be *proud!*"

Todd walked to the front of the line, breathing heavily. "I can do this. The Toddster will sport the short in every port…"

It was the one thing he had been desperately terrified of every time he'd thought about joining up. His hair was his baby, but he knew he would have to let it all go in order to become the man he wanted to be. It was time to be done with being a boy and time to embrace becoming a man.

The team said goodbye to Stephanie's parents as if they were their own. Her mom hugged her tightly and kissed her on the cheek. "I am so proud of you. So proud of all of you. Okay, watching you kick gangster butt was a little hard to take. I won't lie about that. But in the end, you'll take on the world, and you're so wonderful. I wish we could be on Meligorn to watch you receive your medal. We'll watch the television, though, and cheer you on. If you listen hard enough, you might actually hear us."

Stephanie smiled. "I am the way I am because of you and Dad. You taught me to protect what I love, and I love the good-hearted, strong-souled, and kind-minded. So, I think I have my work cut out for me."

Her dad came over and fist-bumped her. "That was the most awesome fight I have ever seen. You were a little terrifying with those black eyes, but hey, everyone has a quirk. I think every one of those gang dudes pooped their pants."

They laughed and she hugged him tightly before she turned and scrambled into the SUV with the team. They rolled their windows down and all hung out to wave and cheer until they faded from view. She laughed, shaking her head at them. They really were her family, and it was so wild to have them.

The next two days felt like a complete and total hurricane. Stephanie and the team returned to Washington so they could get everything they needed packed for the trip. While they were there, they received new armor and the stuff BURT had shipped in because of their new training routine. By the time they were done with trying it on and testing it, they were out of time and had to get the hell out of Dodge and head to Meligorn.

The embassy sent a special bus to take them to the shuttle. Stephanie was placed in the middle and the guys blocked her from being seen through the windows. When the vehicle stopped on the tarmac in front of the shuttle, she used her magic to create a dark-shadowed veil over her face. Her team helped her carry her bags, and they all boarded and settled into their seats in the first-class seating the royals of Meligorn had reserved for them.

Stephanie rolled her shoulders, slipped her arms back into the safety straps, and pushed the locks together over her chest and stomach. She could hear people whispering, some guessing who she was and others knowing only that she was important. Most wondered who the actress was with the entourage of guards.

One woman was so obsessed, she couldn't keep her voice down. "Those security dudes are for real. I can't even think of an actress in this day and age who is that famous. Even amongst the richies."

Her friend whispered a response that made Stephanie stifle a snort. "Maybe she's some royal alien woman and she's here to take our husbands."

The two ladies giggled and the first slapped her friend's hand. "Don't you wish. I'll wrap Ernie up with a bow and send him right along."

The shuttle roared to life around them and the stewardess activated the comms. "Welcome to the 756 Fortune Shuttle headed to Meligorn. Please do not take any items from the lockers until the gravity is activated. Keep your belts fastened at all times. For those that have never been out of the Earth's gravity, you may be tempted to unbuckle and float. Please resist the urge as this can cause you and others injury when the artificial gravity activates. If you wish to experience the weightlessness of space, please speak to one of our attendants, and we'll be happy to take you to the weightless lounge on top of the shuttle. This space is surrounded by glass so you can feel like you are truly floating through the great beyond. In the meantime, please sit back and enjoy your trip."

Stephanie wasn't as nervous as she would have been before

she'd been put through several Virtual Reality simulations of the takeoff and time in space. Still, she was curious as to exactly how realistic the Virtual World had been. The shuttle shook lightly, but not like the early missions where you could barely sit in your chair. The commercial flights were smooth and calm.

The pilot did a countdown and then launched. Stephanie could feel the power of the boosters beneath her as the shuttle inched upward, slowly at first before it increased speed. She held onto the loops on the front of her belt and stared out the window as the world grew smaller and smaller and the sky turned dark.

"Wow," she mused. "Virtual Reality made it seriously lifelike. They did a good job."

Lars looked at her and grinned. "No difference?"

"A little." She shrugged. "Mostly the flipping of the stomach and the butterflies. Everything else seems about the same."

She drew a deep breath and turned to the window to watch as they passed through the upper atmosphere. Then, exactly as she had imagined from the time she'd realized it was real, the gMU began to wind around her, filled her chest when she breathed, and touched every nerve-ending in her body. Her breath fluttered and she grasped the arms of her chair, the feeling amazing and almost overwhelming. The gMU filled the reservoir inside her in a rush instead of a trickle.

Lars tapped her hand. "Uh, Steph?"

"Hmm? she replied and turned to him.

He licked his lips a little nervously. "Is your face supposed to glow under your veil…oh, it's your eyes again. That's a nice silver color, but you might want to turn it off before someone notices."

Stephanie nodded and her gaze slid across the aisle and one row forward. A young child hung over the back of his seat and stared at her, his mouth open in amazement. With a small smile, she waved her hand over one side of her magical veil and canceled it to reveal her face to the child. She winked once before she pulled the magic in and adjusted her eyes to their normal hue.

As the glow died, the child smiled and so did she as she settled in to enjoy the ride. She was headed to Meligorn, a place she'd longed to visit her entire life. It was a dream that had finally come true.

CREATOR NOTES - MICHAEL ANDERLE
JUNE 25, 2019

THANK YOU for not only reading this story but these *Author Notes* as well.

(I think I've been good with always opening with "thank you." If not, I need to edit the other *Author Notes!*)

RANDOM (*sometimes*) THOUGHTS?

I have to say a HUGE thank you to everyone for your kind words about Stephanie and the team.

When I went to the drawing board for a new character, I thought about my time with Bethany Anne of *The Kurtherian Gambit* (*Death Becomes Her* is book 01), and what it was that resonated so much with the readers and me.

Some of those emotions I have worked hard to recreate here (as some have commented) and other stuff I did not. For one, Stephanie doesn't have quite the mouth Bethany Anne has, nor is she as old as Bethany Anne when the story starts out.

I have to admit that I was a bit MORTIFIED when the first book in this series came out.

You see, my company (LMBPN Publishing) had invested a lot of time, money, and effort into putting together the first book, and it wasn't until about two days before release when I realized something...

There weren't that many Fantasy/Space Opera series doing really well.

Not the kind of 'WOW it's selling well!' sales that meant the investment in time and money would come back very fast.

The first day the story made $70.00...then started climbing until it peaked sixteen days later.

At two weeks into sales, I was seeing all of the positive reviews and the climbing sales and realized I had BADLY misjudged how well the book would be received. Fortunately, the sales were in the right direction.

Unfortunately, we weren't in place to be working on the follow up right away, and the group of us had to start scrambling to get this set of stories together. I was up late at Five-50 (a pizza place at the Aria Hotel) typing my little fingers off

Then, the book progressively did better for sixteen days until it peaked in sales at an amazing amount (for me) and slowly started coming down. At this time, it was obvious I had totally misjudged how the readers would enjoy Stephanie Morgana.

By a lot.

So, I immediately pulled the team together, and we started on books 4-6 (ok, that was two weeks later, it wasn't immediate.)

If there was something that could go wrong on the project? *It did.*

We were aiming for the book to come as quickly as possible.

I put a stake in the ground, and we all worked to pull together the stories that I hoped resonated with where I see Stephanie going—her, her team, her friend Todd, and BURT.

Plus the Wonderful Ms. E.

AROUND THE WORLD IN 80 DAYS

One of the interesting (at least to me) aspects of my life is the ability to work from anywhere and at any time. In the future, I hope to re-read my own *Author Notes* and remember my life as a diary entry.

La Puente, CA, USA

I'm hanging by myself, making chili (which my wife can't stand the smell of, so I do it when she is out of town), and I've eaten too much.

I'm like a beached whale that doesn't know when to quit munching on the seaweed.

I'm off to go to sleep now, wishing I hadn't had that last bowl.

I hate myself at the moment, but tomorrow I will be working on that pot again before my wife gets back home.

Because chili is life.

FAN PRICING

$0.99 Saturdays (new LMBPN stuff) and $0.99 Wednesday (both LMBPN books and friends of LMBPN books.) Get great stuff from us and others at tantalizing prices.

Go ahead. I bet you can't read just one.

Sign up here: http://lmbpn.com/email/.

HOW TO MARKET FOR BOOKS YOU LOVE

Review them so others have your thoughts, and tell friends and the dogs of your enemies (because who wants to talk to enemies?)... *Enough said ;-)*

Ad Aeternitatem,
Michael Anderle

CONNECT WITH THE AUTHOR

Connect with Michael Anderle

Website: http://lmbpn.com

Email List: http://lmbpn.com/email/

https://www.facebook.com/LMBPNPublishing

https://twitter.com/MichaelAnderle

https://www.instagram.com/lmbpn_publishing/

https://www.bookbub.com/authors/michael-anderle

www.ingramcontent.com/pod-product-compliance
Lightning Source LLC
Chambersburg PA
CBHW022031120726
47899CB00007BA/2174